MOONLIGHT MADNESS

Moonlight Madness

TALL TALES FROM THE COPPER RIVER VALLEY

SAMME GALLAHER

EPICENTER PRESS
Alaska Book Adventures™
www.EpicenterPress.com

Epicenter Press is a regional press publishing nonfiction
books about the arts, history, environment, and diverse
cultures and lifestyles of Alaska and the Pacific Northwest.

Publisher: Kent Sturgis
Acquisitions Editor: Lael Morgan
Proofreader: Melanie Wells
Cover & text design: Victoria Michael
Cover illustration: Jon Van Zyle
Mapmaker: Marge Muehller, Gray Mouse Graphics
Printer: Consolidated Press, Seattle

Library of Congress Control Number: 2009925604

10 9 8 7 6 5 4 3 2 1
Printed in the United States of America

To order single copies mail $12.95 plus $6 for shipping (WA
residents add $1.70 state sales tax) to Epicenter Press, PO Box
82368, Kenmore, WA 98028; call us at 800-950-6663, or visit
www.EpicenterPress.com.

To Geri and Earle Mankey, who edited my work and helped me out with computer problems. Also, thanks to all those who "spun the yarns" for my stories.

CONTENTS

COPPER CENTER, ALASKA

Rest Stops Along the Richardson

Roadhouse Entertainments

FOREWORD

AUTHOR SAMME GALLAHER HESITATES TO CALL *MOONLIGHT Madness* a work of non-fiction, but a backbone of truth does run through her stories.

Gallaher came to Alaska's sparsely settled Copper River Valley as a teenage girl when that mountainous wilderness was still untamed. She lived in isolated trapping cabins with her sister and brother-in-law. The trio often stopped at roadhouses along the Richardson Highway, then a narrow dirt road, trading stories with trappers and miners, restless travelers, risk-taking adventurers, and a few dangerous misfits.

It is from these people that Gallaher's stories come, in a time and place when lives often depended on the kindness of strangers. Yet, if a man—or a woman—didn't volunteer a name, it was not polite to ask.

If you looked, you probably could find historical accounts documenting many of Gallaher's colorful stories, even if she did not do the research herself. She didn't have to. She came of age in a place where legends were being made, and her stories ring true, borne not just from her creativity but also from her unique Alaska experience.

LAEL MORGAN

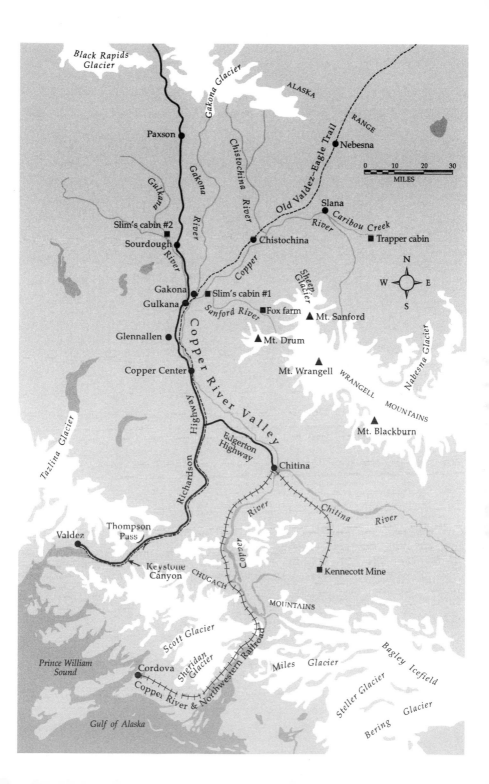

INTRODUCTION

I WAS FIFTEEN THE SUMMER OF 1927 WHEN I TRAVELED alone from my home in California to Alaska. In Valdez, at the end of a steamship voyage from Seattle, I was greeted at the dock by my sister, Aileen, and trapper Slim Williams. They were married that very day in a small church nearby. Then we left for their home on the Copper River.

Our trip from Valdez over the Thompson Pass took us over the top of the mountains. The road seemed to be chiseled out of stone, and we could see the Lowe River below. The road was so narrow that when we met a car coming downhill, someone had to back up to a place wide enough for two cars to pass.

When we left the high road and began to drop down into the Copper River Valley, I had my first view of the place I would call home for a year. It was love at first sight. We arrived at their cabin, settled in, and then set out to do what everyone in the area did for entertainment—we went visiting.

The Gakona Roadhouse, where we picked up our mail, was seven miles away, and we always lingered to visit with anyone who happened to be there. Many times we would chance upon some old sourdough who would be captivating a few awestruck visitors with his tales of the northern woods. The only actual truth we knew about some of those stories was the fact that we'd heard them, but sometimes we knew the tales were true, even though we couldn't vouch for the integrity of the speaker.

In the early 1900s, dozens of roadhouses had been built along the Richardson Trail from Valdez to Fairbanks and in the Nebesna gold fields. They were spaced about one day's journey apart to accommodate the gold-seekers who came by foot or horse-drawn wagon. Many of the roadhouses were little more than small log cabins. Sleeping accommodations usually consisted of one windowless room with cots.

When automobiles began to appear, the trail became a road and eventually a highway. The smaller roadhouses went out of business because travelers could cover the distances more quickly, bypassing the more primitive establishments.

By the time I came to Alaska, the Richardson Highway had been completed, cars were well established, and a stage line furnished transportation for both prospectors and tourists. The roadhouses that survived along the Richardson were at Tonsina, Copper Center, Gulkana, Sourdough, and Paxson. Along the old Eagle Trail were lodges at Gakona and Chistochina, about thirty miles apart. They were all about the same—a hotel, a restaurant, a post office, and a trading post. They were the center of activity along the trails. There were always people at the dinner tables, both locals and travelers, and as often as not the evening entertainment consisted of story-telling.

Tourism was just getting started. Visitors traveled from Seattle to Valdez by steamship, where a driver would meet them with a touring car. Then they would travel the Richardson Highway through the wilderness to Fairbanks, about 360 miles, stopping at each roadhouse along the way.

Rest stops
along
the
Richardson

THERE WERE SEVERAL STORIES
ABOUT CHARLIE. IN ONE, HE
WAS WANTED FOR MURDER.
IN ANOTHER, HE HANGED
HIMSELF IN ROOM 18. I
DIDN'T BELIEVE EITHER,
THOUGH, BECAUSE CHARLIE'S
GHOST WAS SO PEACEFUL.

☾ THE GHOST AT TONSINA

TONSINA WAS THE FIRST BIG ROADHOUSE HEADING NORTH from Valdez. We stayed there one time in the late fall, delayed by a bad storm in Thompson Pass. It was getting dark and raining heavily, so we were glad to pull in. Many other travelers were staying there that night to avoid the storm. The real excitement came after dinner when we gathered to hear tales of the trails, bear scares, and the Tonsina ghost.

"Charlie" is what they called the ghost, seen by many people over the years. He was reported to be a pleasant ghost, and many believed his presence provided an atmosphere of peace and gentleness at the lodge.

There were several different stories about Charlie. One claimed that he was wanted for murder in Canada. When the authorities finally found Charlie, he resisted arrest and was shot. He died in Room 18.

Another version was that Charlie was in despair because a beloved sweetheart had rejected him. Having nothing to live for, he hanged himself in Room 18, and had been wandering up and down the hallways ever since, looking for his beloved. I didn't believe either of these violent accounts, though, because Charlie's ghost was so peaceful.

Later I heard a third version that seemed more credible. During the depression, many young boys were turned out of their homes to fend for themselves because their parents could not feed them. Charlie was one of those boys and had a rough time. He worked when he could, but little work was to be found. One day, in Seattle, he was down by the docks where he noticed a ship getting ready to sail. He asked an officer if he could work on the crew. Fortunately for him, the regular cabin boy had just quit, so they hired Charlie.

When the ship got to Valdez, Charlie decided to stay in Alaska. Eventually he made his way to Tonsina and got a job at the roadhouse.

He loved it. Everyone was nice to him. He was at peace for the first time in his life. Many years later he died alone in Room 18. He was buried on a hill behind the roadhouse. I believe Charlie must be this man's ghost. He had been happy at Tonsina Roadhouse, and surely stayed around because he had no better place to go.

❮ "MA" BARNES AT COPPER CENTER

FLORENCE BARNES OWNED THE COPPER CENTER ROADHOUSE,
the next important stop on the road. They called her "Ma" because
she was like a mother to her customers. Everyone loved her. I was
just a kid when I met her, and she gave me a big, warm motherly
hug. We stopped often at her place. Copper Center was the hub
of the trails and it seemed like the center of our world. There was
always someone to visit with. After you'd been in the wilderness
for awhile, it was wonderful to talk to another human being.
Meals were served family style on one big table that accommodated
ten or twelve diners at a time.

After the table was cleared, the adults played a card game
called Panguine, or "Pan" for short. I didn't play, but often
watched until I could hardly keep my eyes open. Ma usually
was in charge of the game, dealing out the cards so precisely
that they plopped right down in front of the players in neat
piles. Gambling would go on until the early morning hours almost
every night, except Sundays.

On one quiet evening, Ma told us why she had come to Alaska. She was born in New Zealand and became a nurse. She loved her work, but in a terrible influenza epidemic, she almost died caring for the sick. It was so hot that even those who were ill left their homes by the hundreds to sleep on a high hill in hopes of catching a breeze. The unbearable heat killed more people than the epidemic. This was a horrible experience. When the epidemic was over and life went somewhat back to normal, Ma decided to find a new life in Alaska where it wasn't so hot. She bought the Copper Center roadhouse and ran it with the help of her man, Bill.

Bill was a drunk, as we called them in those days. This was during prohibition, but booze was not too hard to find. Ma kept her supply hidden under lock and key, not from fear of the law, but for fear Bill would get into it. Once we arrived to find Ma was boiling mad, screaming at Bill because he had consumed a bottle of vanilla extract just for the alcohol in it.

At that time, only two people lived near the Copper Center roadhouse—Paul White, the wireless operator, and his sister, Merle. Their little house was the equivalent of about two city blocks away. The local population increased between spring and fall with the arrival of road-construction gangs.

We went to many dances during the summer. They were always a big event in the valley, and they usually ended in the same way. There were about five men for every girl, and before the last dance was called, someone usually took a poke at someone else who had "cut in," and the dance would end in a fist fight. Those who went home without loss of blood considered it a good night.

It may be hard for someone who has never lived in the wilderness to understand how important the roadhouses were.

After a winter in a small log cabin, usually alone with your dogs, it was exhilarating to go to the roadhouse to see and talk to anyone there! Even though there were three of us—Slim, Aileen and me—we yearned for other company. At least once during the long winter months, we would hitch up the dogs and hit the trail to visit Gulkana and Copper Center.

# GULKANA

THE GULKANA ROADHOUSE WAS OWNED AND MANAGED BY Mrs. Elizabeth Griffith and her daughter, Mrs. Anna Leak. It was not equipped for more than one or two guests, and the women did not serve big meals. However, it was still important to the people in the valley, more as a trading post than a roadhouse. One could buy hardware, such as shovels and axes, and other supplies. We always stopped there on our way south to Copper Center.

☾ SOURDOUGH

HEADING NORTH ON THE ROAD, THE NEXT ROADHOUSE WAS Sourdough. It had been an important stop in the early days, but "Doc" Blaylock, who lived there, did not manage it as a going business anymore. It was completely run down, and by the time I got there, no one was stopping. After Doc was gone, however, it was restored and reopened.

 PAXSON

PAXSON, NEXT, WAS ONE OF THE BUSIEST ROADHOUSES because it not only served travelers but also boarded local residents. Dan Whitehead managed Paxson, and I loved to visit in the summers when his daughter, Mrs. Meggitt, and her three teenage children—Danny, Grace and John—came to help Dan during the busy season.

At that time, Paxson was an overnight stop for a touring company out of Valdez, and passengers usually arrived just before dinner. After eating, the tourists listened to local trappers tell stories about "life or death" at fifty degrees below zero. I remember one night when the story-telling went on until two o'clock in the morning.

 GAKONA

THE ROADHOUSE CLOSEST TO OUR CABIN WAS AT GAKONA. A good road had been built over to Gakona from the Richardson Highway, and it continued on for about twelve miles, ending right in the middle of the woods. The original roadhouse was built in 1904, but a newer and larger Gakona Lodge was built next to it in 1924 by the Norwegian owners.

Operated by Arne Sundt and Herb Hyland, Gakona's newer two-story building offered furnished guest rooms with two shared bathrooms upstairs. Our post office was in the corner room off the huge lobby. Meals were served in the original roadhouse next door.

One year, Arne Sundt went back to Norway to find a bride, and he found one. The next year, a girl named Audra made the journey alone all the way from Norway. Arne met her in Cordova and they were married the same day in a friend's home. They raised a family at the Gakona roadhouse—one of the first, if not the first, white family in the Copper River Valley. When Arne died, Audra continued to run the business by herself for many years.

☾ CHISTOCHINA

CHISTOCHINA WAS THE ONLY ROADHOUSE BUILT IN THE wilderness, with no road access, although the old Eagle Trail to the Nebesna country ran close by.

"Red" Hurst built and managed the roadhouse—a large, primitive building made entirely with logs and having no modern fixtures. The sleeping room in the attic was a big open space with a few cots for men. Accommodation for women consisted of a small, walled-in corner room on one side of the attic with one window and one bed. We often stayed there, and Aileen and I would sleep in that little ladies' bedroom. There was no room service, of course, and I suspect the bedding—two heavy blankets—had not been changed since the place opened. We cautiously slept with all our clothes on, even our hats and gloves, although we did take off our shoes.

Despite these shortcomings, Red surely cooked the best pot of beans I ever tasted. We stayed many times at Chistochina on our way to Slana, heading up the Chistochina River. But something happened the last time we slept in the attic room that was unnerving.

It was in late September and a strong wind was blowing as Aileen and I climbed up into the attic. We got into bed, pulled up that filthy blanket, and went to sleep. About an hour later, I was awakened by what sounded like a baby crying. I nudged Aileen.

"It sounds like a baby crying, but I think it's only the wind," she said.

We tried to shake it off. But we heard the sound again, and then it would be quiet, and if we tried to sleep, again we would hear the sound of an infant crying in the dark. Of course by then we were wide awake.

The next morning at breakfast, we asked Red what we had heard. He stared at us for a moment. "I suppose it was the wind, but it is strange that only women hear that sound," he said thoughtfully.

"The native women who have heard that sound believe it's the ghost of a baby who died in childbirth up there many years ago," he recalled. "I don't believe in ghosts myself, and I've never heard it. Once I tried to find out if the wind was making a sound in that room. I chinked up all the spaces between the logs and thought I'd solved the problem. It's been years since anyone reported having heard anything strange."

Before we left that day, Red asked us not to talk about what we had heard. We were the only white women who had heard the crying, and he didn't want a ghost rumor to get started. We agree and said nothing to anyone about Chistochina's ghost. But that was the last time we stayed in the little room. Now, after all these years, when I think about what we heard, tears still come to my eyes.

I cried, too, when I read that the Chistochina roadhouse had burned down. The thought that I never would see it again saddened me. Another roadhouse eventually was built nearby. Red Hurst ran it for years and then moved into the Nebesna country with his wife. Did the new place have ghosts, too, I wondered? What happens to ghosts when a place they haunt burns down?

Most of my roadhouse experiences made wonderful memories. It was fun hearing those wilderness tales told by the odd mix of people who claimed to have lived them or to have known first-hand the people who had. I think of my treasured story collection of that bygone era as a rich tapestry of human experience.

ROADHOUSE ENTERTAINMENTS

THE SHOCK OF THE FIFTY-BELOW
TEMPERATURE HIT ME LIKE A
PUNCH IN THE GUT. I STOOD
STILL FOR A FEW SECONDS
TRYING TO CATCH MY BREATH
IN THE SUFFOCATING COLD

☾ FREEZING FAST

WHEN IT'S DARK IN THE WILDS OF ALASKA, IT'S REALLY DARK.
On such a night, with no moon reflecting light on the snow and
no stars shining in the heavens, there's nothing else to raise even a
glimmer of light. It's so black that you truly can't even see your
hand held out in front of your face. At the same time, there's a
strange stillness in the brush. Nothing moves around out there. The
darkness seems to compel almost all the animal life to remain
completely silent.

It was on just such a night that I had my first real experience
with the darkness and cold. Our thermometer registered fifty below
zero, and that's what started the whole thing. The cold was like an
invader trying to get into the cabin, and all we could do was huddle
close to the fire. I felt hemmed in—this was "cabin fever"—and I
began to complain about the miserable night.

Well, my sister Aileen and her husband Slim listened to me for
a bit, and then Aileen began to read us a story. But I couldn't get

interested in it, and neither could Slim. A feeling of uneasiness overwhelmed our small cabin.

I'd received a newspaper in the mail from my mother full of lovely sepia photographs of Los Angeles—snow-free streets, lofty palm trees, and scenes of swimmers at the beach. The sunny glow of the hills filled me with a longing to be there. I had made two trips in my young life to the city of L.A., and I'd been enthralled by its beauty. So I began to talk about Los Angeles, and how I would love to live there.

Aileen listened politely, and went along with the thought of living there, but my brother-in-law, Slim, would have nothing of it. He began trashing L.A., saying it was full of awful people—crooks, robbers, molesters, and every other evil thing he could think of. "It's hot in the summer and hot in the winter and nothing in between. You can't get a good job there because they don't have any trade unions, and workers get peanuts for their work. No, I wouldn't live there if they *gave* me the danged place."

From experience I knew Slim was going to keep his tirade going for a while. I wanted to yell back at him. What did I care about trade unions? I just knew it was a lovely place to live. As he ranted on about that beautiful city, I began to get hot under the collar, and it wasn't because of the stove. He was making me angry.

At first, I tried to argue with him, but it was no use. I was just a 'yap-kid', as he called me, and he was master of all things in that wilderness of the north. But he kept on and on, making me feel like a fool for even thinking of living in L.A., until finally I stood up in a huff, held my head high, and marched out the front door.

The shock of the black night and the fifty-below temperature hit me like a punch in the gut. I stood still for a few seconds trying to catch my breath in the suffocating cold, and then walked away from the cabin. I wasn't ready to go back inside, defeated, so I decided that as long as I was outside, I'd go to the privy. As I picked my way through the snow, I realized it was too dark to manage this little trip without a lantern, so I turned back to where I thought the cabin should be. But I had lost my sense of direction, and suddenly I tripped over something and fell. I must have hit my head, because I blacked out.

When I came to, I felt something wet and sticky on my face. I tried to brush it away but my right arm was pinned under me, and I couldn't move it. When I began to move my left arm, I felt something warm and furry lying on it. Well, it didn't take me long to realize it was our big old dog, Beaver, licking my face. I tried to move him, but he wouldn't budge. It was about then that I heard Slim calling me from a long way off, but I couldn't answer with Beaver licking my face.

Aileen and Slim had laughed at me for going out and had waited about ten minutes for me to come rushing back in. When I did not return, they thought I was fooling with them and began calling. Finally, they became alarmed. I'd gone out with no wrap of any kind, and by this time I'd been outside about fifteen minutes. At fifty below, a person starts to freeze in that time and lose the ability to function.

Realizing something was wrong, Slim lit a lantern and Aileen grabbed some coats and blankets. They looked for me close to the cabin at first, calling over and over. Aileen became hysterical, and Slim yelled at her to calm down.

I had hit my head on Beaver's dog house and fallen down behind it. I couldn't be seen, not even with a lantern. When Beaver saw Slim, he began barking. By this time I was stiff from the cold and could hardly move. Slim lifted me up and as he carried me into the cabin I could see he was close to tears.

I didn't win the argument with Slim about Los Angeles, but I did shake him up a bit. I don't think he'd ever been around a teenager before. He didn't realize that I had a mind of my own. He treated me with a little more respect after that night, and actually admitted begrudgingly that L. A. probably wasn't as bad a place as he had said.

Speaking of respect, I came to have more of it for the dangers of being out at fifty below!

FIRST GAKONA ROADHOUSE

BEN TRIED TO JUMP ACROSS THE
CREVASSE BUT DIDN'T MAKE IT. HE
HIT THE EDGE, AND FELL INTO THE
CRACK. THAT RIPPED THE ROPE
RIGHT THROUGH MY HANDS . . .

 # BUGGY

"WHAT A GOD-FORSAKEN COUNTRY."

Old "Wheezy" Birch muttered these words as he came into the screened porch at Tonsina roadhouse and sat down beside me. It was a hot day, and he was wiping off his sweaty face with a dirty red bandanna.

I laughed and said, "Why, Wheezy, I thought that this was the land you loved. You're always bragging about how wonderful Alaska is. What changed your mind?"

He chuckled, loosened the top button of his shirt, mopped off his neck, grinned at me, and replied, "Well, nothing changed my mind. I still love it, but I don't love this gol-derned heat and the blasted bugs. They just drive me nuts."

I could see when he opened his shirt that he still had on long johns. I said, "For gosh sakes, Wheezy, no wonder you're so danged hot—you've still got on your winter underwear!"

"Oh, man, I never go without them, come summer or winter. What would I put on under my pants?" he replied.

That was the end of that conversation, as other folks had come into the porch to cool off.

Wheezy Birch had come north a few years before the big Gold Rush, and he was the oldest "old-timer" in the valley. When he arrived in Alaska, he was just a kid, but already knew how to hunt. He had been raised in the woods of South Carolina and could shoot the head off a squirrel at age eleven when he had gotten his first .22. He'd even had a little business selling squirrels for twenty-five cents and rabbits for thirty-five, fully cleaned and dressed. When asked if he had gone to school, he replied, "Yep, but only when I had to."

I don't know how he got the name of Wheezy, but it must have had something to do with his voice. He got a kind of high-pitched whine after he talked for a while. And he was famous for his talking. No one could spin a yarn better than old Wheezy.

Wheezy had been well known as a guide for big-game hunters. Then, the hunters stopped coming and Wheezy worked at anything that helped feed him. He freighted with dog teams, carried the mail, panned for gold, trapped in the winter, and helped Mrs. Franks at Tonsina Roadhouse.

This day he came into the screened porch to sit for a while after Mrs. Franks had told him to get out of the heat and cool down. He was driving her crazy. She'd had enough of both Wheezy and the bugs for one day.

"Guess you never expected to see California sunshine in Alaska, did you?" Wheezy was talking to a young hitchhiker.

"No, sir, I didn't. I never thought it would ever be this hot in Alaska, and I surely didn't expect all these bugs. I bought a net to cover my face, but they get to me anyway. What do you do to get rid of them?" the young man asked.

"Well, that's a hoot," said Wheezy, slapping his knee. "How do we get rid of them? We don't! The main thing is learning how to live with 'em. That reminds me of a partner I had once. His name was Ben Charles, and he hated them bugs. During the bug season, he was as mean as a bear, and came to hibernate like one of 'em. He actually 'holed up' and didn't move around much during the worst of the bug season.

"He used to say how he could put up with the swamps being wider, the tundra heads higher, the brush thicker, the air hotter, the trail longer, or even getting hisself rain soaked—if only the pesky bugs would just lay off. I guess he meant it all right, 'cause he quit hitting the summer trail and built hisself a log cabin, with a big screen porch where he could live free of the bugs. I seen him burn four moss smudge fires at the same time, and him in the middle cutting wood. His cabin door was in smoke range of the woodpile. All he would do was sit all day and read or just sit and smoke his pipe. He explained that if he got up steam, he would have to eat, and eating meant cooking, and cooking meant firewood, and firewood meant cutting it, and that meant getting out among the pesky flying critters.

"There was a yellow insect powder called buhac. You'd sprinkle it on a fire and it would send up a smoke that'd kill the bugs. It cleared 'em out for a spell, but more'd just come back. Nothing much you could do to get rid of them dirty little critters. That buhac smoke was almost bad enough to kill a man. And so it went—man against bug, bug against buhac, and buhac against man. You just couldn't win for losing.

"At first, I come to think that Ben was just plumb lazy, but come fall and winter he was out and about doing all kind of things. He had a little hand-drawn sled that he used to pull in his logs for firewood. Also, he ran a trap line by hisself. We asked him why he didn't get a few dogs to haul for him and he always said, "You got to feed 'em, and I don't want that problem."

By this time, others had come out on the porch to cool off and when they heard old Wheezy telling one of his tales, they stayed put. Wheezy would hesitate in his story just long enough for a newcomer to settle down. Then, when we all gave him our undivided attention, he would continue.

"There was one summer when we prospected together. We had found a secret valley, and it was hard to get to. It was between a range of low hills and a glacier. The small glacier cut it off from the flat land, so we had to cross the glacier or go miles around it to get to this valley. A stream was running from the side of the glacier down to a little swampy lake in the bottom of the valley, and it was just waiting to be panned. We discovered it on a trip we took a few years before, and we'd planned to come back and get some of the yellow stuff.

"One day, after hitching my five dogs to a small sled filled with our grub, blankets, axes, and pans, we headed out on the April crust. There was still some snow, but it was thawing fast and by the afternoons it was soggy and hard going, 'specially for the dogs. So, we'd break camp about four in the morning after the trail had crusted overnight, and then we'd slip along until afternoon, by which time the sun had softened the trail again.

"We had fair going the day we crossed the glacier, but we had to get across while it was still daylight. We was plumb lucky that it was cloudy and cool, 'cause the sun didn't do much thawing. There was a few crevasses, but the snow and ice bridges over 'em were still frozen. Still, we'd always test 'em before we'd cross. By the afternoon, the going got real easy, but, I can tell you, we was sure glad to get down off that glacier and stand on good ol' Mother Earth again!

"From then on the going wasn't too bad. The valley was flat and open. It took a couple of days to find a good place to build a cabin. We found a high spot above a little creek where the cabin would be hidden behind a thick stand of spruce. There was still plenty of prospectors roaming 'round Alaska and we didn't want to be seen. It didn't take us long to throw together a little log shack. Then we hunted game and found plenty of it. We got all the sage hens and rabbits we needed to feed us and the dogs. While there was still a little snow left, we harnessed up the dogs and they pulled in enough firewood logs for the season.

"We was busy for a time cutting them logs into firewood, and getting set for the work we came to do. By this time it was May, and soon the water began to run. From then on we was busy as beavers in the creek. We was getting a little color here 'n' there and a real good pan once in awhile. There was plenty of daylight by now, so we'd work as long as we could until we was tuckered out, then we'd go to the cabin to rest our bones.

"Everything was going along real fine until June came along with her hordes of mosquitoes. They didn't bother me too much, but they about drove Ben crazy. I knew he hated the bugs, but I never knew how bad it was until he began cussing, clawing the air, stamping his feet, and running around in circles. He said that created a breeze to blow them gol-darned bugs away. He'd stand it as long as he could, and then he'd run to the cabin and stay there until I came in. I knew he didn't do it to get out of work, 'cause he would always have a meal ready.

"Well, this went on through July and the middle of August. By then all the bugs in Alaska was buzzing around. The gnats, the flies, and them big horse flies were driving us buggy. The moose flies were the worst. Where a mosquito only sticks you, the moose fly actually takes a bite right out of your flesh. Nothing you put on it will ease the pain and the itching. Out in the brush, the mosquitoes follow you in a black cloud and cover your net so thick you can't see through it.

"Now, by this time Ben was a case. He was almost crazy with fighting them bugs. We thought to stay there 'til October and find a different trail back to Tonsina, working our way around the glacier. It would take us longer, but the bugs would be gone to roost for the winter.

"Ben didn't want to wait. He begged to go. He wanted to be in a house he could walk round in and be away from the bugs. He almost broke down and cried. I reminded him that the bugs would be gone in October, but that made no difference to him. He just wanted to leave. Well, I figured he was about on his last legs, so I agreed to leave that very evening. We'd panned enough to do us 'til the next spring, and anyway the water in the creek was gradually getting lower every day.

"We couldn't use the sled without snow, so I made some packs for the dogs out of a tarp and loaded them up with what little we had to take with us, along with the dog harness, which I couldn't part with. We left our working gear cached in the cabin, so we'd have it there when we came back next summer. The dogs were almost too fat, but they were raring to go as soon as I put packs on 'em.

"We had a couple of miles to go up the main stream toward the glacier, and then out onto a flat plateau. From there we could see to the left the low gap we'd go through. Beyond that was a string of swamps and lakes 'til we came to an old Indian trail that would take us to the Copper River, and then we'd just follow the river to Tonsina.

"Well, I might have known. Ben wanted to keep on going up the valley and skip across the glacier. 'Skip across the glacier' is just the way he said it.

"There we stood! The dogs ready to go, mosquitoes humming hopefully, gnats crawling all over us, flicking their wings, dancing around looking for holes in our nets, or gaps in our shirt fronts to crawl into, even poking their noses in button holes.

"'Ben, for God's sake, what do you mean 'skip across the glacier'?" I asked. "'You know it'll be tough going this time of year. It'd be dangerous for us--you know that--and how about the dogs? This other way would only be about fifty miles through the swampy area and then out onto easy traveling.'"

"Ben jabbed his finger at me and said, 'Yeah, I know what kind of trail that'd be. It means swamps, tundra heads and yeller water lakes, and them along with all the gnats, mosquitoes, and—if it don't rain—them gluttony moose flies. I tell you, Wheezy, I can't stand no more. Let's go over the glacier. It's up high and it'll be a breeze.'"

"I just couldn't believe Ben wanting to go across that glacier. I shook my head and told him, 'Sure, there's like to be a breeze, even one enough to blow all the bugs away, but Ben, you sure do know what the ice would be like this time of year —the sun beating on it, it'll be like greasy glass and as full of holes as a sponge.' "

"But Ben just went on about the bugs. 'Their danged infernal singing and getting on my veil, so's I can't see. I'd not last one day in those swamps. I know I'd just go nuts.'

"Well, I said, trying to reason with him. We got a few swamps the other side of the glacier, what about them?"

"'But at least we'll be a lot closer to getting out of here when we do get across,' he argued.

"'You're right about being close to something,' I argued back, 'Closer to hell in a cake of ice, and where'd the dogs be?' "

"Ben looked real puzzled for a bit, and then he said, 'Let's go back and get that rope we used to hang meat on, we can use it on the ice. And let's leave a couple of days' food behind, we won't need it, and that'll lighten the dogs' packs.'

"Well, I can tell you I was about to just forget Ben and go on by myself, but dang it, partners have to stay together. Breaking up on the trail is a real bad thing to do. So I turned 'round and we headed back to the cabin.

"We got the rope, took out some of the food, repacked the dogs, and started out again. I admit that I grumbled about what we was doing, but Ben was cheerful, and even hummed a little. We finally got to the glacier and found a way through some small crevasses up to where we could cross. Ben was right. There was a nice little breeze, just strong enough to blow them bugs off of us. But we had another problem. The sun was well up by the time we'd started again, and it was busy melting the ice. It made the ice so slippery that we could hardly stand up, so we wound a dog chain around each foot. That helped some.

"Finally we came to a crevasse that Ben and me could jump across, but it was too wide for the dogs. So we found a thin snow and ice bridge, and we figured we could help 'em over on that. First, I tied the rope around my waist and jumped across, then I threw the rope back to Ben. Ben took off the dogs' packs and threw them over, and then he'd tie the rope 'round a dog, right behind its front legs. I'd call the dog, and it'd come across to me. The dogs seemed to get the idea and did just what I told 'em. It was something to see 'em walk across that bridge real careful. I've found, after years of driving 'em, that dogs can just read your mind. They know when there's trouble.

"When we got the dogs across, I threw the end of the rope back to Ben and he sort of wrapped it 'round his wrist to have a good hold on the end, while he jumped over. But what happened at that crevasse still leaves me shaking when I think about it. Ben jumped and didn't make it. He hit the edge of the crevasse, slipped back, and fell into the crack. That ripped the rope right through my hands, but I managed to catch a knot at the very end of it."

Wheezy paused for a grim reflection. No one on the porch said a word. We all just waited for Wheezy to catch his breath and go on.

"Ben yelled as he fell. I stood there for a second before I looked down. Ben was only about eight feet down, but he was in a bad spot. He was squeezed into a narrow crack, and his body was twisted. One arm was pinned under him, and it looked like he couldn't turn enough to free it. His body had sort of turned over as he fell, and I saw that he'd have trouble getting that arm free. But his other hand still had hold of the rope.

"Ben began shouting, 'Get me out of here! Pull me outta here!' I pulled, and he yelled again, 'Oh, Jesus, that hurt. Wait a minute—I'll try to move around. When you pulled, it really hurt my back I'm twisted.'

"I could see he was struggling to move, and finally he freed his arm and got out of that cramped position he'd been in. 'Now try to pull me again!' he yelled.

"I pulled, slipping and sliding, and couldn't move him even a little. I yelled, 'I've got an idea, Ben! Just try to hold still for a bit.'

"Well, I was mighty glad I'd been stingy enough to keep my dog harness. I got it out of the pack and onto the dogs as fast as I could. Then I had to tie the ropes from the harness to Ben's long rope. All this time Ben kept yelling, 'For God's sake, hurry up! I am getting wedged in tighter with every breath I take.'

"I worked real fast, 'cause I was scared he'd squeeze down farther to a place where I could never get him out. But I just kept telling him that we was gonna get him out.

"After I got the ropes all tied, I told the dogs to tighten the lines, and then I yelled 'mush!' The dogs jumped and pulled and slid on the ice, and I pulled 'til my eyes bugged out. Ben screamed in pain. I told the dogs to rest a second. Then I called to Ben, 'Let me know when to pull again.'

"'Oh, God, it feels like you're twisting me in two!' I could see that he was free from his hips up and told him to get the rope under his arms. When he did, I yelled, 'Mush!' again. With those five dogs and me pulling as hard as we could, out of the jaws of ice came Ben, up over the edge. We dragged him clear from the crevasse before I yelled 'Whoa!' to the dogs. I often wondered how we did what we did that day, with so little footing for the dogs."

Everyone on the porch, including me, heaved a sigh of relief. Someone called out, "What happened then, Wheezy?"

"Well," he continued, "Ben sat there on the ice for a little, took off the rope, and felt all over his body. Then he smiled and said, "Well, I guess nothing's broke."

"But when he stood up, he began acting strange. He didn't want to go on; he wanted to stay right there, arguing that there wasn't no bugs there. Talking wouldn't convince him that it was a crazy idea, so I repacked the dogs and started to walk away. He followed, but then stumbled and fell. He got up again and tried to walk, but finally he just sank down, begging to camp right there. I figured he must be hurt, so I got an arm around him and supported him, pulling him across the glacier until I had to rest.

"Suddenly he began to laugh, and said he'd played a good joke on them bugs! Then he yelled at me to pull him out, that the ice had got him. I didn't know what to think, so I called to the dogs to move on, and what do you know, Ben got up very meekly and followed us! The rest of the way over the glacier wasn't too bad. There was no more wide crevasses to jump over. We just plodded along and didn't talk much. But when we got down off the glacier we was in swamp country, and here come the bugs swarming around us in clouds. We cut a small leafy tree branch to wave in front of us, to help keep them dang bugs out of our face. Ben was crazy by then and I guess I was getting there myself. The poor dogs were miserable.

"Finally we dragged into a friend's cabin, and were we ever relieved to be out of the bugs for a while! We filled up on eggs and fresh baked bread. They sure tasted good after the hard tack we'd been eating since April.

"Then we had about fifty more miles to go to the roadhouse. We had bugs—not as thick as they was in the swamps, but there was still plenty of 'em. Ben was quiet most of the way, except for fighting and cussing the bugs. Once he asked me about what had happened up on the glacier. He couldn't remember if I'd fallen in, and he'd pulled me out, or was it him who fell, and I'd pulled him out? When I explained that the dogs had saved him, he laughed and said, 'I'll bet I'm the only man whose life was saved on a glacier by five sled dogs.' "

"It was a big relief when we got to Tonsina. No place had ever been a more welcome sight. A few days later, Ben left Tonsina headed for his own cabin, and I only saw him once after that. It was the next summer, and I dropped by to see him in his bug-proof cabin. We never spoke of our glacier trip. In fact, we didn't even mention working the little creek. The supplies we left are still up there, and if any of you ever stumble onto our little cabin, help yourself."

With that, Wheezy stopped talking. He dropped his head down and put his hand up to his chin as though he was thinking about something. He looked around the room at his audience, which by then had grown sizeable, and said, "The bugs! I got to get out of here 'fore they come. I bet I can beat 'em to my cabin."

With that, he jumped up, ran out of the porch, and made off into the woods. We sat there for a few moments, stunned by Wheezy's abrupt exit.

Then Mrs. Franks came out and announced, "I've got to tell you all something about Wheezy. He loves to tell that story about the glacier, and we always listen, but Wheezy's never been the same since Ben and those dogs pulled him out of the crevasse. He probably hit his head. It seems that the trauma of the fall, along with all those bugs, made Wheezy just a bit buggy himself."

LOBBY - COPPER CENTER ROADHOUSE

ONE NIGHT WE HEARD A WOLF
HOWLING QUITE CLOSE BY. IT WAS
UNUSUAL TO HEAR JUST ONE WOLF
HOWL. I THOUGHT HE SOUNDED
SAD, AND WONDERED WHY HE
WAS ALONE.

CALL FROM THE WILD

My sister, Aileen, lived in Alaska for six wonderful years, and had many stories to tell. She told me this story with tears in her eyes.

JUST NORTH OF WHERE THE SANFORD RIVER FLOWS INTO THE Copper River, the remains of an old log cabin rest in peace. Part of the roof has caved in, and a cache, once perched high up on stilts, has tumbled over. The trees and brush almost hide it from view, but my memories of that little home on the Copper River are still clear.

Those were happy years. I loved my life in the wilderness with my husband Slim. But what I loved most were my dogs and my timber wolf. Yes, I had a full-blooded wolf, taken from a den just after his eyes were open. He was a delight from the moment I saw him. He was scared of everything in our new world, and when he trembled, I held him in my arms and mothered him.

When the man who had given him to me came by to see how we were getting along, he saw the wolf hopping around. He laughed and said, "Let's call him 'Hoppy'," and Hoppy it was.

I had Hoppy chained to a big tree right in front of the cabin, so I could watch him. A slip chain at the bottom of the tree made it possible for him to move around the tree, and I called that area "Hoppy's circle."

Most of my leisure time over the next two years was spent watching my wolf. At that time, little was known about the wolf's behavior and nature. Wolves had been depicted in literature in a negative way. But watching Hoppy, I knew he wasn't bad. He was affectionate, and loved to be petted and talked to. When there were pups running around, you should have seen Hoppy mother and father them! He was as gentle with a puppy as a human parent is with a baby. He would lie still when a puppy wanted to cuddle up to him, and remain quiet until the pup moved.

Few people ever knew about Hoppy's lovely odor. When life at the cabin was in complete harmony, with no turmoil of any kind—no wind, no rain—just peaceful, Hoppy emitted a sweet fragrance, sort of a musky, earthy smell. It came right off on my hands when I petted him. Only three other people ever had the pleasure of smelling Hoppy's "perfume."

My main reason for accepting the wolf was to mate him with a couple of my dogs to get some half-wolf pups. So, when he reached the age when most canines are ready for parenthood, I expected that Hoppy would be ready, too. But he would not mate. No one knew then that only the alpha male and female in a wolf pack mate. It was not until a year later that I took Stub, our faithful mother, into his circle, and she managed to seduce Hoppy.

When their four pups were born, you should have seen him. It was evident that he knew the difference between his pups and any others. What a parent he was! When his pups were weaned, he fed them by regurgitating his food, and he got very thin during that time. He played with them most of the time, and as they got bigger, he taught them how to fight. But never once did he hurt any of them.

Three of the pups were the same color as their father—a yellowish gray—and one was deep black. The black one was beautiful, but he had a defect. His left ear did not always stay spiked up like the other. Most of the time, it sort of sagged forward a little, but when he got excited, it would stand up just like its mate, so I named him Spike. I figured he got that ear from his flop-eared mother, Stub.

He was so different from his sisters. They loved to play, but Spike preferred to stick close to me. I kept him close and put his bed right by the front door. Each night before I turned in, I petted and cuddled Spike. Although his sisters Copper, Gypsy, and Wrangell loved to be petted, too, Spike seemed to have an unusual need for human affection. I loved all the dogs, of course, but Spike had a special place in my heart. (Spike's three half-wolf sisters later were part of the sled dog team that mushed in 1933 all the way from Copper Center, Alaska, to the White House in Washington, D.C. But that's another story.)

At any rate, one night we heard a wolf howling quite close by. We often heard the call of the wild, but always at a distance. Besides, it was unusual to hear just one wolf howl. The pattern generally was that when one started, right away the others would join in. This one wolf, howling so close by, sounded sad and I wondered why he was alone.

Two days later, down by the river, I saw a movement in the brush near the bluff. I saw enough to tell that it was a gray wolf. He appeared to have sat down and he was looking at me. I saw only his head and shoulders, but I knew he was a big one. I was not afraid of wolves, as I had never heard of anyone being attacked by one, but I did not linger. Back at the cabin, I got down my rifle just in case that wolf came after one of my dogs.

The next day we heard that lone wolf again. He was back in the same place I had seen him before. He sat there for a few hours every day for about a week, howling intermittently. Then he stopped his vigil, which is what it seemed to be. This was a relief as I felt sorry for him, and his presence somehow made me apprehensive.

Meantime, the dogs had been restless, and when the wolf howled, they howled, too. The wolf pups seemed frightened and stuck close to Hoppy. Spike would nestle close to his father, or come to me.

Then, one night a month later, we heard that mournful howl again. In the morning there he was, sitting and watching.

One night a week later, something disturbed the dogs. They weren't barking loudly, but they were whining and growling. I opened the door to look around. There was plenty of moonlight. Although I saw nothing, Hoppy was restless, running around in a circle while the other dogs had climbed on top of their houses.

I called to Spike, but he was not there! I found his collar. It had not been chewed or cut. He had managed to pull out of it, and I realized I had been so anxious not to make it too tight or uncomfortable on his neck that it must have been too loose. I called for Spike the rest of the night, but he never came. My darling Spike was gone.

The gray wolf was gone, too, and he never came back. I examined the area where the other wolf pups slept, and from the evidence, it appeared that they too had struggled to get loose from their collars. Had their collars been as loose as Spike's, they probably would have run off as well. All day long, I walked up and down the river, calling for Spike.

That night I cried myself to sleep, fearing that I would never see Spike again. I cried every day for weeks and vowed never to become so emotionally involved with an animal again.

That winter, a strange thing occurred on the trap line. The little cabin where we stayed during trapping season was close to a creek. We had cut a trail up to a ridge leading to the trap line. To the left, across a deep ravine, was another ridge. On this particular morning, Slim had gone up to the trap line very early. I followed him later. When I reached the top of the ridge, I saw that I had company—a pack of wolves on the next ridge. I had heard them howling for days, but had thought little of it. Now they were in full view. I just kept on going, and as I moved along, they went in the same direction. They would race on ahead, stop, and start howling. They seemed to be playing with me.

This went on for a mile or so. Then, out of curiosity, I stopped my dogs to see what the wolves would do. I had a good view of them and spotted two black wolves. "What if . . . ?" I asked myself, and so I just began calling, "Spike! Spike!"

One of the black wolves separated from the pack and stood looking in my direction with his head held high, listening. He wasn't close enough for me to see if his left ear flopped, but I kept calling. Suddenly he turned and ran back into the pack, and away they went, down the other side of the ridge and out of sight. I never saw that pack again.

Was that Spike? I could never prove it, but in my heart I knew that it had to be. Could he have heard a call from the wild? Had that big gray wolf come to call the pups and Hoppy home?

For the rest of the years that I lived in Alaska, the howl of a wolf always brought a lump to my throat.

BELOW, IN A TINY OPENING
BETWEEN TWO LAYERS OF
CLOUDS, WAS THE LITTLE TOWN
OF VALDEZ. THE PILOT DESCENDED
IN SPIRALS UNTIL THEY BROKE
OUT INTO THE CLEAR.

 A BEAVER TALE

WHEN ALASKA WAS A TERRITORY, THE RULES, REGULATIONS, and laws came from the federal government, even though many of the men who made those laws never had stepped foot in Alaska. In 1925, the federal government established the Alaska Game Commission. Many of the rules it wrote were regarded as a joke. For instance, one law seemed to say that you could not kill a bear unless it was molesting you, and even then, you had to write the government and get permission to protect yourself.

Another law limited trappers to ten beaver skins per season. The skins had to be inspected by a federal agent, who then would stamp each skin with an official seal. The seal had to be stamped on the skin side of each fur before the trapper could sell it, and possessing an unsealed beaver skin could get you into trouble.

This is a story about two young fur trappers and six unsealed beaver skins.

In 1930, Slim and Aileen lived on a bank of the big river seven miles upriver from Gakona. During the long winter, the river was a frozen highway for travel by dog team from Gakona up to Chistochina and Nebesna. There was a stopping place along that river trail—Slim and Aileen's cabin. Travelers were always welcome to come in for a cup of tea, a slice of Aileen's home-baked bread, and a friendly visit.

One day, two friends, Paul White and Allen Smith, stopped on their way to Copper Center. They had trapped that season up in the Chistochina area and were in high spirits. It had been a good season, and they were bragging about how many fox skins they had. They were bursting to show off their bounty, so Slim and Aileen went out to see what they had. When they pulled back the canvas covers on their sleds, Slim saw not only the fox skins, but also beaver skins beneath them. He reached down and pulled one out, held it up, and said, "Where in hell did you get beaver skins? There's no beaver up where you were trapping."

"Yeah, that's right," said Paul, "but we didn't trap them."

"Well, where'd you get 'em?" Slim asked.

"From old Chuck Wallen. He told us he'd trapped them last year. Just before trapping season, Chuck took ill, so I went over and took care of him. Chuck turned out to be mighty sick, and was getting worse and worse. I sent word up to the Kennicott mines for Dr. Gillespie, but he couldn't come down.

"Chuck got delirious and began mumbling, but all I could make out was something about beaver skins. Allen heard him too. Both of us figured he wanted me to take the skins to pay for all I had done for him. Allen had helped out with Chuck on occasion, so I gave him two skins and I kept four."

Slim shook his head and said, "Paul, you and I have been friends for a while, and I never expected you to do such a damn fool thing as taking those skins. Chuck didn't really give them to you, did he?"

Slim then inspected the skin more closely, looking for a seal. He couldn't find one and said to Paul, "Evidently, Chuck didn't declare these skins to the Game Commission, 'cause I can't find any seal on this one. You know you can't sell 'em without the seal. Besides that, have you got any proof that Chuck meant for you to have them? ... I'd advise you to take 'em back."

"Oh, no!" protested Allen, "We earned those skins. Chuck was hard to take care of, and we lost some trapping time helping him."

"Well," said Slim, "it's your business, so do what you want. What did you do with Chuck after he died?"

"Well, at first we didn't know what to do," Paul said. "I knew that Chuck was real good friends with Red Hurst, 'cause he'd been out there to see Chuck a couple of times. So I thought maybe Red would know what to do. I stayed there with Chuck while Allen went to the roadhouse, but then he came back alone. Red was gone. Allen left a note at Chuck's cabin telling him about Chuck being dead. We couldn't just leave him there, so we went over to the native village and found two men who knew Chuck to come help us. We loaded him onto the sled and took him over to an old burying ground. I found a couple of stones to mark his grave. It was hard digging through that frozen ground. Then we went back to our cabin, packed up, and started down river."

With that, Paul and Allen covered up their sleds, yelled "Mush!" and were on their way. Slim stood there shaking his head. As they walked back to the cabin, Aileen laughed and said, "Those two nuts are bound for trouble."

Meantime, Red Hurst, who ran the roadhouse in Chistochina, returned to Chuck's cabin and read the note from Allen. Once before when Red had been out to see Chuck after he took sick, Chuck had told Red that if he died, Red was to take the beaver skins in payment for what Chuck owed at the roadhouse. He'd even signed a note to this effect. So, when he heard that Chuck had died, Red went out to the cabin to pick up the beaver skins.

When Red found that they were gone, he was sure they had been stolen. He knew they'd be worth about $250, just about enough to pay off Chuck's debt. So Red notified the government agent, C.D. Cadwalleder, in Copper Center. He explained that the beaver skins were rightfully his, and that his proof of ownership was a signed paper from Chuck.

Cadwalleder went to Chistochina to investigate. On his way upriver, he stopped at the Williams' cabin. He explained that Red Hurst had reported six beaver skins stolen from Chuck Waller's cabin after Waller's death, and that he was looking for the thieves. Cadwalleder asked them if they had seen anyone pass through recently, going down river.

Slim and Aileen weren't surprised to hear that the beaver skins were thought to have been stolen. Slim told the agent that Paul White and Allen Smith had stopped on their way to Copper Center, and that he and Aileen had seen beaver skins in their sleds.

"Paul told us that Chuck Wallen died, and that he had taken the skins in payment for taking care of him during his illness. I don't believe he thinks of them as stolen," Slim told the federal agent.

With that information, Cadwalleder issued arrest warrants for Paul White and Allen Smith. Paul was arrested in Copper Center. Allen could not be found.

Slim and Aileen didn't know any more about the affair until Ma Barnes at Copper Center told them that Paul had been arrested on suspicion of theft and was being held in Valdez. Then, a few days later, they received a subpoena to testify before the Grand Jury in Valdez.

Unfortunately, at that time of year, traveling from the Copper River Valley to Valdez was easier said than done. Thompson Pass was still closed, so Harold Gillam, the local bush pilot, was hired to fly them to Valdez. That turned out to be a dramatic journey.

On May 2, 1930, Aileen and Slim climbed aboard Gillam's Swallow Aircraft, an open cockpit biplane. Aileen was wrapped in a bearskin robe and Slim in a blanket. They took off from the small Copper Center landing strip, but did not get far. The coast was completely socked in with clouds and fog, forcing them to turn back. The next day they tried again. Again, they failed to reach Valdez. On the third day, they were able to get much closer to the coast, although it was still hidden under a heavy cover of clouds. Aileen and Slim searched for signs of a landing strip, but there was only whiteness as far as they could see.

Suddenly Gillam knocked on the side of the plane to get their attention. There, below, in a tiny opening between two layers of clouds, they saw the little town of Valdez.

Gillam descended in spirals until they came out in the clear over Valdez. No one was expected to be flying in that kind of weather, so the markers for the landing area on the beach had been removed. Gillam circled the town until they were hurriedly put back in place. Then he made a bumpy but safe landing. Aileen and Slim were a little shaken, laughing nervously at the risk they'd taken just to appear before a Grand Jury.

Slim and Aileen and C.D. Cadwalleder were the only witnesses to appear. Aileen and Slim's testimony was simple— they had seen beaver furs in the possession of the accused men. Paul White and Allen Smith were indicted.

White was already in jail. But when Allen heard that Paul had been arrested, he had made himself scarce. Authorities finally found him in Gakona, where they arrested him and flew him to Valdez.

Both men appeared before the district court on May 12, and were charged with the theft. Paul White pleaded guilty. He was taken back to jail to await sentencing.

Allen Smith entered a plea of not guilty, which meant there would be a trial. Bail was set at $500, and a trial was set for a week later in Cordova. The U.S. government subpoenaed the witnesses, which of course included Slim and Aileen. When they received a notice to appear at White's trial, Slim lost his temper. "Who in hell does he think he is? He knows we saw the skins, and he's guilty as hell. Now we'll have to go to Cordova, and stay there for days."

It was a hardship to be gone, what with their yard full of sled dogs, puppies, and one timber wolf. If they couldn't get their friend Mike Cotter to take care of the animals while they were gone, one of them would have to stay behind. Luckily, Mike was able to help, and a good thing, too, because they were gone for many days.

Getting to Cordova was a lot safer than a trip to Valdez. They drove to Chitina, left the car there, and took the train to Cordova. It was almost like a vacation.

On May 20 at ten o'clock, twelve jurors were seated and the trial began. Slim and Aileen found the court proceedings to be amusing. Allen may not have stolen the furs, but he took his share from Paul, who had taken them and who had pleaded guilty. The defense attorney was trying to prove that Allen was not a thief, just an accomplice.

After a few witnesses testified, Slim and Aileen were called to the stand. Aileen was questioned first, testifying that she had seen beaver skins in Allen's sled. After he was sworn in, Slim attempted to sit down in a very small chair provided for the witnesses. Moving it back so he would have room to sit down, Slim toppled it over, and everyone in the court room roared with laughter. The judge pounded on his desk to demand silence. Slim picked up the chair and said, "Hope I didn't break it." Everyone laughed again except the judge, who pounded on his desk again.

Slim gave his testimony, and the defense did not cross-examine him. When Slim went back and sat down beside Aileen, he leaned over to her and whispered in his loud voice that carried to the whole courtroom, "Now, can we go home?" The judge pounded.

There was a lot more legal jargon exchanged between the plaintiff's and defense attorneys before the trial was recessed.

The next morning, just as the session began, the defense asked for a "demurrer." Slim leaned over and in his loud whisper asked Aileen, "What in the hell is a demurrer?" Of course she replied, "How should I know?" The judge then pounded his desk again and declared sternly, "If we have any more loud whispering, I will clear the courtroom."

Anyway, all that they learned about a demurrer was that it didn't come to pass. After more witnesses were called and more legal rigmarole that seemed unimportant, Paul was called to testify. Paul had a difficult time answering the questions that established Allen had taken some of the beaver skins. At one point, when Paul seemed as if he was about to cry, Slim leaned over to Aileen and loudly whispered, "Damn, I wish he'd listened to me and returned those blasted skins!"

The judge banged his desk again, pointed to Slim, and said to the bailiff, "Remove that man." This pleased Slim, who went outside and rolled himself a cigarette.

Court was recessed after Paul's testimony. When the trial resumed the next day, the judge instructed the jury to begin deliberations. It didn't take jurors long to return a unanimous guilty verdict.

All that remained was sentencing. Three days later, the judge sentenced Paul White and Allen Smith to be imprisoned for one year in the federal penitentiary at McNeil Island, Washington. In addition, Smith was to pay $230 in court costs. Then, the judge suspended the prison sentences and adjourned the trial.

Neither man would go to prison.

Paul and Allen were free to go. They both lived in Copper Center and boarded the train to Chitina. Aileen and Slim went home on the same train. When the train was about to pull into the Chitina station, Paul sat down across the aisle from Slim. He stuttered a little and asked Slim if he would give him and Allen a lift to Copper Center.

"Well, let's see." said Slim. "If you promise not to rob Aileen of the beaver collar on her coat, we'll take you home."

Aileen began to laugh under her breath and then Slim laughed out loud. Paul looked embarrassed for a moment but when he saw the humor, he laughed, too. Finally Allen, who had been at the other end of the car, joined in the laughter. When they got off the train and loaded their luggage into Slim's car, they were all still laughing.

I LOVED TO GET THE PUPS HOWLING
BY HOWLING MYSELF. THEY SOON
JOINED ME IN A CHORUS OF HOWLS.
BUCKY TRIED, TOO, BUT ALL THAT
CAME OUT WAS "BAH, BAH, BAAAAH."

☾ WHAT HAPPENED TO BUCKY?

WHEN OUR PUPPIES WERE BORN AT THE COPPER RIVER cabin, I was in seventh heaven. I loved them all, but especially Bucky, who was the most unusual pup we ever had.

He did not behave like a pup. He did not walk like a pup. He just plodded along as if life were a burden. He stayed off by himself, and never played with the others in his litter. We named him after a comic-strip character.

I could pet and cuddle any of the pups except Bucky. He didn't like to be touched. He would become rigid, tighten his legs out straight, and act as if he was going to be killed. I used to pick him up to see if he would become accustomed to being held, but he always stiffened up.

Bucky was pure white. He didn't have one spot of color on him. His four siblings were colorful. Patagonia, his brother, had long, bushy gray hair. Bracken, his sister, was a little beauty with shiny, short black hair, and Goldie, another sister, had semi-long, silky yellow hair. The prize of the litter was Rembrandt.

He was gray and white and had a quiet manner. When I picked him up for the first time and saw his lovely face, he reminded me of a Rembrandt painting. So we named him after the painter, but we called him Brandt for short.

These five pups were unusual in that they all were so different from one another. Often products of the same litter will have something in common—color, texture of fur, or shape. What these pups shared was a love of romping, except for Bucky. He would watch them play and then turn away and find somewhere quiet. He was fond of Hoppy, our tame timber wolf, and liked being close to him. If Hoppy was lying down, Bucky would snuggle up to him and sleep.

I loved to get the pups howling by simply howling myself. They would follow my lead and soon join me in a chorus of howls. Bucky would throw his head back and try to howl, too, but instead of a howl out would come "Bah, bah, baaaah." Then he would look around and look sheepish, no pun intended.

One lovely fall day, my sister Aileen and I took a walk up the trail along the Sanford River leading to George Bellefontaine's fox farm. All five pups followed us. They were four and a half months old and full of vitality. As we walked, they would run ahead to explore. Then, we would pass them and after awhile here they would come, again, running ahead of us. But not Bucky. He just plodded along in the rear.

We turned back after hiking about two miles. By then, the pups were dragging their heels far behind us. At the cabin, we waited and finally four weary pups came down the hill and into the yard. Bucky was not with them. At first I didn't think anything about it, but after an hour, I became alarmed. I went back up the trail, calling Bucky. I felt sure that he'd show up, but he was still missing at bedtime. I slept poorly that night.

Next morning, I walked back up the trail, calling again, but with no response. After a couple of days I was told to forget him. Finally I gave up. We were convinced that he couldn't have survived alone for more than a day or two. Even though Bucky was an oddball, I loved him, and I was saddened to think about what might have been his fate.

Ten days later, the pups suddenly began barking. I went out to see what the fuss was about. There, coming down the hill was Bucky, limping and walking slowly. When I tried to pick him up, he cried out. The lightest touch seemed to cause him pain. He had no breaks that I could see, though it was impossible to examine him closely. He had some grimy spots on his fur, possibly blood mixed with dirt. When I fed him, he gobbled his food so fast that he choked on it.

It took a few days for Bucky to get back on his feet, but he was a different dog. He still didn't play with the other pups, but he was in full charge of them. If they were playing and a fight broke out, Bucky stopped it. They recognized his self-made authority, and he ruled the roost, so to speak, even though he still preferred to be with Hoppy.

He grew up to be a strong sled dog, a hard worker and always alert and obedient. But he still didn't like to be touched. His body always seemed tender, so it was difficult to get him into his harness. But once we got it on, the harness didn't appear to bother him.

We never did figure out what happened to Bucky. We always suspected that an eagle had picked him up and for some unknown reason dropped him in the woods far from the cabin. But we never knew for sure, and Bucky wasn't saying.

HIGH IN THE TREE, MRS. SQUIRREL MOVED CAUTIOUSLY TOWARD THE END OF THE BRANCH. HELD TO HER CHEST IN HER MOUTH WAS A NESTLING. THE BRANCH SWAYED LOWER AND LOWER.

SCOLDING FROM MRS. SQUIRREL

IN 1927, THE DIRT ROAD FROM GAKONA TO THE EAST WAS CUT out of the brush for about thirteen miles. From the end of the road it was seventeen miles to Chistochina.

One beautiful summer day, Slim, Aileen, and I decided to hike up to Chistochina. We had a couple of pack dogs along to carry our gear knowing we would be gone for a few days. We left Gakona early in the morning and hiked to the end of the muddy road. From then on the going was easier than walking through the mud, even without a road

By afternoon we were slowing down and were ready for some hot tea and a snack. We stopped at a small stream. The spruce trees were large and gave us plenty of shade. As we began to build a small fire, a squirrel began to chatter and scold us from the branches of a spruce tree above us. We were intruders.

In gentle tones, we tried to explain that we didn't wish to disturb her, and that we were sorry about the fire. We told her that we wouldn't stay long, and asked her to be patient. She seemed to consider our plea for a moment, but then continued her noisy complaining.

We couldn't see her, but as we sipped our tea, we noticed that the branches above us were moving about, revealing some activity. Occasionally Mrs. Squirrel would dart into view and demand, "T-t-a, t-t-ta, t-t-ta, t-ta, t-ta!" Obviously, we were taking too much time for lunch.

Finally, after a long silence, we guessed that she'd given up her quarrel and departed. But we were wrong, for suddenly our attention was directed to a long swaying branch, high in the tree. Mrs. Squirrel was moving cautiously toward the end of the branch. Held to her chest in her mouth was a baby squirrel. The baby was larger than a nestling, and although it seemed too small to travel, it also seemed too large for Mrs. Squirrel to carry easily. After every tiny step, she readjusted her baby with her forepaws. As she neared the end of the branch, it swayed lower and lower. Fully three feet from her was the flimsy branch of another tree. She edged out farther, jiggled for firmer footing, adjusted her load one last time, and leaped! When she landed on the targeted branch, it dipped sharply down and then up and seemed unsteady. But Mrs. Squirrel clutched the limb firmly while holding her baby.

Well, we began to breathe again, and were glad to think that she was going to a new home free of intruders. However, our relief didn't last long, as we watched her return to her former home, then fly two more babies from tree to tree!

We hoped she would be content in her new home, but to our surprise, once again we heard her defiant, nagging chatter.

After all, we were in her part of the woods, and she wanted us out!

As we walked away, my heart was filled with a deep sense of respect and love for all the wild creatures on this Earth, a respect I hold dear to this day.

SUDDENLY, I HEARD WHAT SOUNDED LIKE AN EXPLOSION. THE WHOLE MOUNTAINSIDE OF SNOW LET LOOSE WITH A ROAR AND LOUD WHOOSHING SOUND AS AN AVALANCHE CRASHED ONTO THE TRAIL BELOW.

THE GHOST OF GAKONA HILL

Many people told this story up and down the road, but Mike Cotter's version was my favorite. He was an old trapper who lived near Gakona, and was a great story teller.

ONE COLD, FROSTY NIGHT WITH THE MOON PEEKING through high windswept clouds, giving just enough light to see the trail, I mushed my way down to the Gakona Roadhouse. I had stopped my team at the top of the hill to be sure no one was on the trail ahead. Once we started downhill, it would be hard to stop. Suddenly, just as I was about to kick off, I heard an eerie sound in the still night.

At first, I could not figure out where it came from. But after listening more intently, I realized it was the sound of another sled dog team on the trail behind me. But somehow it sounded strange. I looked back fully expecting to see dogs approaching. Through the icy mist, I saw nothing. Yet, the sound came nearer, and the hair on the back of my neck stood up. I could hear a team nearby, but I saw nothing.

Surprisingly, my dogs became quiet and tense. Usually they had to be held back when another team approached. Now, each one stood perfectly still. My little black malamute, Klute, issued a frightful whine. All of a sudden, the sound of this phantom team came right alongside of us. I clearly heard the words "Mush, Zag!" and the sound of a sled sliding by on the ice and snow as it barreled down the hill. Then, the sounds faded into the night, and once again it was quiet.

After I calmed down, catching my breath, we proceeded cautiously down the hill. I was certain that there was a team ahead of us, and I didn't want to tangle with them. But when we got to the roadhouse, there was no other dog team to be seen. I went inside and asked Herb, the proprietor, if another team had stopped. He scratched his head, and said, "No one else has come in tonight. Why do you ask?"

"I thought for sure that I heard a team go down the hill ahead of me. I even heard the driver say, "Mush, Zag." Do you know anyone with a leader called Zag?"

Herb stood with his mouth open for a moment and said, "You know, there used to be a trapper named Zolt who lived way up on the Gakona River. He had a dog named Zagreb. We used to tease him about the name. He would laugh and say that was the name of the city in Yugoslavia, where he was born. He probably called his leader Zag, but other than that, I don't know of any other Zag."

"Does he still live up there? Maybe that was him I heard last night, and I just couldn't see him through the mist."

"Oh, no, it couldn't have been Zolt. He and his dogs disappeared five years ago. A strange Chinook had softened the river ice that winter. When Zolt didn't show up for supplies and mail, I became concerned and went up to check on him. He and his dogs weren't there, so some of us hereabouts started a search along the river.

"Part of his sled was found caught in some brush below his cabin. We searched high and low but no trace of Zolt or his dogs was ever found. We were sure he had gone through the ice after the Chinook."

Herb and I stood there looking at each other nervously for a few moments. Then Herb said, "I think we'd better have a cup of coffee and I'll stoke up the fire. It feels cold in here."

We had our coffee and talked about the phantom team I had heard. Herb was as puzzled as I was. After getting my supplies and mail, I headed back up the hill.

A couple of weeks later I went to the roadhouse again. When I stopped at the top of Gakona Hill, as I always do, I heard—but did not see—a team coming up behind me again. I waited as it drew near, excited to learn more about the phantom team. Once again I heard the driver call out to his leader as the team drove by.

Then, just as I was about to start down the hill, I heard a sound like an explosion. The whole mountainside of snow let loose with a loud roar and a whoosh as an avalanche crashed down on the trail below. I could hardly believe my eyes.

Had I not stopped for the phantom team to pass, my dogs and I would have been half-way down the hill, buried deep in a mountain of snow.

I DIDN'T THINK I BELIEVED IN
GHOSTS, YET I HAD NO OTHER
EXPLANATION FOR THE INVISIBLE
VISITOR THAT THE DOGS WATCHED
INTENTLY AS IT MOVED AROUND
THE YARD.

THE SPIRIT OF STICK

This story relates one of Aileen's experiences with the dogs. They had become the center of her world in the wilderness.

MY AUNT ALLIE LOVED TO TELL GHOST STORIES AND SCARE THE daylights out of my sister and me. She said the Sugar Man was a ghost living in her attic. If we got into the sugar, she said, the ghost would "get us"—whatever that meant. This was during the World War I, when sugar was rationed, and I'm sure this was her way to keep us out of the sugar bowl. She made me deathly afraid of the Sugar Man and all the other ghosts she told us about.

We were told that the Sugar Man had long, brown, thin legs that spread out like a spider and big ugly teeth. His black stringy hair hung down over his legs, and he crawled around in the dark ready to grab us. Well, he never got me. As the years went by, I outgrew my belief in ghosts, although to this day I do not put sugar in my coffee.

Years later, something strange happened that made me rethink my views on ghosts.

My life changed when I married Slim, a fur trapper, and went to live in the wilds of Alaska in his little log cabin on the Copper River. A team of nine sled dogs was our transportation, and those dogs became my greatest interest. They were all different breeds, varied in appearance, and complete individuals. One thing they all had in common was their love of being petted.

Slim warned me not to pet the dogs too much, however. He explained that these were work dogs, not pets. A kind word and a pat on the head were permitted, but that was all if I wanted to drive them. Well, learning how to drive the dogs was my greatest desire, but I couldn't stop myself from petting them.

Each morning, I would make my rounds, talking to and petting each dog. When I opened the cabin door, they knew I was coming, and they jumped on top of their houses with wagging tails held high.

As I got acquainted with them, I noticed that one dog named Stick was different from the others. Whenever I talked to him, his response was amazing—he really seemed to understand what I said! I fell in love with Stick and gave him more attention than I did the other dogs. I couldn't resist. Slim noticed this and warned me not to give one dog special attention.

Life on the banks of the big river was a storybook existence— no rush, no worries, and no deadlines to meet. The days were tranquil, filled with the beauty of nature, and, of course the dogs. I had been there four months, getting used to this paradise when stark, grim tragedy struck.

One of Slim's customs was to turn the dogs loose for a run every morning. As they were untied, they ran off in all directions. This day, Stub, our leader, dashed into the brush behind the cabin with some of the dogs following her. The others went off in the opposite direction. Stick was always the first one to come back, and when he did he looked for me.

One day, Slim and I decided to cut a new trail down to the river. The work could be done in a couple of hours as the brush was not thick. When we got ready to start, three dogs—Stick, Blue and Sonki—had returned from their morning run. The other dogs were still out. Slim chained the three to their posts, and we left. If only we had taken them with us. I had a bad feeling and didn't want to go, but I said nothing.

Later, on our way home, Slim began to worry. He realized that he'd made a mistake chaining the three dogs. It was possible, he said, that the other dogs might have returned from their run and attacked Stick. His remark shocked me, and I felt a sense of dread.

When we came into the yard, we saw Beaver and Brindle sitting by Stick, covered with blood from their muzzles to their shoulders. They watched him intently, ready to pounce again if he moved. But Stick would never move again. They had killed him. Having been chained, poor Stick never had a chance to defend himself.

Oh, God, was I responsible for his death? Slim had warned me about playing favorites, but I didn't listen. I covered my eyes and burst out crying. Slim caught me as I began to collapse. He led me into the cabin and told me to lie down.

"I'll take care of Stick, you just stay in here and be quiet," Slim said. I lay there for hours in anguish. How could I love these dogs as I did, when they were capable of such unrestrained violence?

The tragedy broke my heart, and I could think of nothing else. Whenever I went into the yard and saw Stick's empty house, my eyes filled with tears. My heart ached for his charming ways and intelligence. I had learned a hard and bitter lesson. From then on, I would follow Slim's instructions about handling the sled dogs.

A week after Stick's death, I was alone in the cabin when suddenly I heard the dogs bark and whine as they did when someone was coming. I went out to see who it was. The dogs all stood on their houses wagging their tails, their eyes moving in unison as they watched something walking around the yard. However, I didn't see a thing. Then, one of the dogs acted as if another dog had approached and was greeting him. A second dog did the same. It was as though something was walking from one dog to another.

Although the sun was shining brightly, there was a sharp chill in the air, and I had an eerie feeling. The dogs watched whatever it was come toward the cabin, stop for a moment, and then turn toward the river. The dogs settled down.

I had watched this amazing occurrence for almost five minutes. I swear the dogs had seen something that was invisible to me. When I went back inside, I shivered as I sat down and tried to control myself. What had the dogs seen? My thought, of course, was Stick.

I didn't think I believed in ghosts, yet I had no other explanation for the invisible visitor that the dogs watched intently as it moved around the yard. Stick was such a good dog. Maybe he wanted to say goodbye. If there are human ghosts, wouldn't dog ghosts exist, too?

Paxson Roadhouse

FROM THE CORNER CAME A LITTLE
SOUND. HUDDLED ON THE FLOOR,
WRAPPED IN A BLANKET, WAS A
YOUNG NATIVE GIRL. SHE TRIED
TO SMILE, BUT I COULD SEE SHE
WAS FRIGHTENED.

☾ TWO STRANGERS

When I lived with Slim and Aileen Williams in a cabin on the Copper River, a man named Dan Turner stopped by. He wanted to visit the cabin where he had lived years before, and he was eager to tell us about his life there. He told us this story.

AFTER THREE MONTHS OF NOISE AND CLAMOR IN WHAT MANY call civilization, I stood on the deck of the *S. S. Alaska*, sailing home from California. I watched until the lights of Valdez came into view, eager to get back to my beautiful Copper River Valley. It was the end of August, and that's a great time to be in Alaska. Days were still warm from the late summer sun, and the mosquitoes had gone to their winter homes. Fall colors were beginning to appear in the woods, and the deep blue skies were often full of whipped cream clouds.

At three o'clock in the morning of August 9, 1922, the steamship tied up at the dock. I got my gear together, walked down the long wooden dock into town, and went into the lobby of the old Golden North Hotel. The drowsy night clerk moved slowly as he checked in the new arrivals.

Late the following morning I awoke to typical Valdez weather. It was overcast with rain, but it felt good to be on Alaska soil again. After breakfast, I bought a winter supply of food staples, loaded them into my old Reo, and headed north on the Richardson Highway.

The steep road over the Keystone Canyon was a challenge to my old touring car with its heavy load. The Worthington Glacier peeked through the clouds, and soon the sun cleared them away. Before long, the road dropped down into the Copper River Valley. The Richardson was not the best road in the world, but it went through some of the most beautiful country in my world.

Having been away all summer, I was anxious to see my dogs and my old pal, Mike Cotter, who had fed them while I was gone. I looked forward to resuming our regular cribbage games, although Mike was not much competition.

I had traveled to Seattle in July to help celebrate my mother's eightieth birthday. My siblings had come from all over the country. It was a joyous time seeing them again after so many years. We all had gone our own ways, and it was a great reunion except that my ex-wife Agnes, who had remained close to my mother, was there, too.

Our marriage had failed from the beginning. Agnes resented everything I stood for, and I never understood. So I just walked away one day without even saying "So long" and a year later sent her a card from Valdez, Alaska. She obtained a divorce on the grounds of desertion.

Now that I was on my way home to the valley, I felt happy and carefree, without anyone or anything to worry about. I enjoyed being alone. I suppose I am a loner. I wanted to live by myself in the wilderness with my dogs, trap in the winter, fish in the summer, loaf in the fall and spring, maybe visit Mike once in awhile.

The old cabin stood in a clearing by the Copper River, at the bottom of a high bluff. Because the path to the cabin was steep and narrow, I didn't have many visitors—and that was just the way I liked it. After parking in a clearing at the top of the bluff, I turned off the engine and listened to the sound of my barking dogs. They had begun their clamor the minute they heard my car. The sound was music to my soul. These dogs were my life.

On my first trip down to the cabin, I greeted my dogs with affectionate petting. When I had gotten my first dogs, someone told me that you could pet them, or drive them, but you couldn't do both. Well, that is an old trappers' tale. I learned to do both.

Hauling down the supplies took a number of trips. Once the goods were stacked in the log cache, the late afternoon had turned cold, and I was eager to get inside the cabin and build a fire. It was at that moment that I noticed a wisp of smoke coming out of the chimney. Someone had built a fire, but whom?

If someone was in the cabin, why had they not made themselves known? Surely I had made enough noise to be heard. It couldn't be Mike. He would have come out the minute the dogs began their serenade.

I hesitated, feeling apprehensive, and then opened the door slowly, calling out, "Hello, anyone here?"

From the corner came a little sound. Huddled on the floor behind a chair, wrapped in a blanket, was a young Native girl. She was staring at me, and tried to smile, but I could see she was frightened. For a moment or two we looked at each other, and then I said, "Well, where did you come from?'

She didn't reply, but when I stepped toward her she began to whimper. I stopped, leaned down to her and said, "Don't be afraid of me. I'm not going to hurt you. I only want to know what you're doing here in my cabin."

She stopped whimpering and finally, in a barely audible voice, whispered, "Mike, he bring me here. He got me out of the river."

"Out of the river? What on earth were you doing in the river?" I asked.

"Me and Ewan go down the river, and he fell in the water. He went under and not come up. Then Mike grabbed me out of the river." She began to cry and through her tears said, "What I do now?"

I felt sorry for the child. "Please don't cry," I said. "I see that you've had a bad time here, and I'm sorry that you lost your friend. But why did Mike leave you here alone? Why didn't he take you with him?"

"He say I can't go up the hill." And with that, she stood up, pointed to her stomach. "My baby come soon. Mike say you take care of me."

"He did, did he?" I said, but I was thinking, "My God, what on earth do I do now?" I struggled for the words to calm and reassure her, but I needed calming and reassuring myself.

Instead, I said, "I'm as hungry as a wolf, and I'll bet you are, too."

A pot of beans simmering on the stove looked mighty good, so I filled a couple of bowls. I handed one to the girl and asked her, "I'm Dan. What do I call you?"

"My name is Manny," she replied, as she took the bowl and sat down.

"What were you and Ewan doing on the Copper River? It's dangerous even for the best river man."

"Oh, we need to go far away. Our home up in the Yukon, but we leave. Ewan kill my father. We go away before Mounties come take Ewan. We never go back."

"But you could go back, you didn't kill anyone," I said.

Manny shook her head and began to cry again. "My people not want Ewan and me. They say he bad, and his child be bad, too."

I asked her why her husband had killed her father.

"My father hit my mother real hard, and she fall down," Manny said. "He start to hit her again, and Ewan hit my father on the head with big stick. My father fall down and die. Then we run away.

"Ewan found old boat on bank of river. He said we go fast on river. It was good 'til we go into big river. We go too fast and Ewan stood up with oar to push the boat back away, but boat hit bank. Ewan fall into fast water. His head bob up. I never see him again. I grab boat, and Mike pull me out of water." When she finished her story, Manny was trembling.

What could I say? She had just lost her father and her husband, and almost her own life. "Okay, Manny, you're welcome to stay here until Mike and I can figure out what to do."

When it was time to go to bed, some changes had to be made. Manny had been sleeping on my bed, and I needed to make a place for her. There was enough room between my bed and the wall to make another bed on the floor. She sat wrapped in her blanket, watching me. When that was done and the fire was built up for the night, I pointed to the new bed and said, "You sleep here."

When I awoke the next morning, something was amiss. I didn't know what until I heard Manny fixing the fire. Oh, yeah! Now I remembered what was wrong. What in tarnation was I going to do about her?

That afternoon Mike came to feed the dogs. He was glad to see me, but I was not so happy to see him. As he came into the yard, I blurted out, "What the hell do you mean by taking this child into my house and telling her I'd take care of her?"

Mike laughed. "Well, I knew you'd help a lady in distress." It was a big joke to him.

"You did, huh? But apart from that, how did you get down to the river in time to help Manny?" I asked.

"Well, I glanced up the river just in time to see the boat swerve over into the deep, fast channel. I knew they'd be in trouble, and I got down there just in time to grab the girl. The man had been standing up, when the boat hit the bank. He fell over into the swift current and disappeared. Another second, she'd have been gone, too.

"I had a hard time getting her out of the water and onto the bank. She had on lots of wet clothes, and with her big belly, she was awful heavy. I couldn't carry her until I pulled off her wet coat and some shawls she'd wrapped around her shoulders.

"She's been here now for about two weeks and we've become good friends. I think that Manny is about fifteen or sixteen. She's afraid of what will become of her and the baby. So, I told her you'd take care of her. Good God, man, you can't turn her out! She's got no place to go and no people here to help her when her baby comes."

I thought about it for a moment. "I guess you're right. She can stay for now, but what about the baby? Hell, I don't know anything about delivering babies! I know about dogs—they never seem to have any trouble--but women, I don't know much about them."

"Don't worry about that, Dan. My old lady had five kids and I helped every time. She never had any trouble, much, so just keep your shirt on."

As the weeks passed by, I got used to having Manny in the cabin. She could make a fire, cut up caribou for stew, and cook beans. Most of the time, she hummed a little tuneless song. Strange as it seems, I began looking forward to seeing her when I came in.

Manny always seemed happy to see me. She listened to me ramble on, smiling and nodding her head.

On October 5, 1922, Manny gave birth to a scrawny, wrinkled baby boy with a hint of red hair. She screamed a little but didn't have any trouble birthing the baby. Mike helped during the birth. Afterward, he wrapped the baby in a blanket, handed it to me, and announced, "Here's your baby."

"*My* baby? What do you mean, *my* baby?" I exclaimed.

"For one thing," Mike replied, "the boy has a tint of red hair and even though your hair is almost white, your beard is sort of red. With Manny living here, and the baby's red hair, people will think he's your boy."

"Maybe so, but where do you suppose he got that red hair?"

When the baby began to cry and squirm, a powerful feeling came over me. As I held him in my arms, I experienced a sense of love for that child, and I never let him go.

Manny named him Danny after me, and from then on, my life was centered on my two little strangers. They were my children, Danny and Manny, and they brought a true sense of family into my life. With two children to father and nine sled dogs to care for, life took on a new meaning. This loner was no longer alone.

Now, if I can just teach Manny how to play decent cribbage, my life will be complete.

IN A ROTTED KNAPSACK, A WOMAN'S
BRUSH AND COMB WERE BARELY
RECOGNIZABLE. THE ONLY THING
INTACT WAS A SMALL WHITE JAR WITH
"COLD CREAM" EMBOSSED ON THE
LID. HAD SOMEONE DIED HERE?

☾ A PIECE OF RED RIBBON

George Bellefontaine was the only Frenchman living in the Copper River Valley. He had a fox farm up on the Sanford River about five miles from the Williams' cabin. He stopped at our place on his way home, conveniently arriving around dinnertime, and he loved to tell tales. Of all his stories, this is my favorite.

EACH YEAR IN THE EARLY FALL, BEFORE THE SNOW COMES, I hike up to my trapping cabin on Caribou Creek at the foot of Mount Sanford to get it ready for the trapping season. The two-day hike with Beaver and Patagonia, my two biggest pack dogs, feels like a vacation. I follow pretty much the same trail each year.

One year, however, I decided to go up the Sanford River first to visit George Bellefontaine, my closest neighbor.

When I left George's place to head for my trapping cabin, I cut across an unfamiliar patch of woods a couple of miles south of my usual route. I came across a small clearing and was surprised to see that a campfire had been made there some time ago. This was a remote area with visitors and I wondered who might have camped here. It couldn't have been George. He hates camping.

I decided to stop for the night. As I gathered firewood, I was startled to find a tiny bit of red ribbon tied to the branch of a tree. I took it down, examined it closely, and saw that it was a piece of red ribbon tightly wound around some metal hairpins. The pins had been pulled out straight and then twisted together, end to end, until the thin piece of metal was long enough to fasten securely to the tree. It looked as if some little creature had nibbled on the ribbon.

Below the ribbon, almost hidden by leaves, was a tin cracker box wedged between two branches. Evidently it had been tied there with a fragment of rope. I pushed away the surrounding brush and found some camping gear and two rifles. In a rotted knapsack, a woman's badly chewed brush and comb were barely recognizable. The only thing intact was a small white jar with the words "cold cream" embossed on the lid.

I was puzzled. Why were the rifles and personal belongings so important to a female left behind? Could someone have died here?

I took the cracker box down from its place in the tree. The lid was difficult to remove. Inside, I found a small paper tablet, old and brittle. I opened it carefully. On the first page was written "My Trip." This is what I read:

PLEASE READ WHAT HAPPENED HERE.
June 1905

Today, as I write this entry, I am alone in this wilderness. I came to Alaska to find my brother. He left home five years ago to find gold, and since then we never heard from him. After I arrived in Valdez, I went from roadhouse to roadhouse along the trail to Fairbanks. I asked everyone if they knew my brother. I found a man at Copper Center who said he knew him and the mine where he worked. Todd

Braden was the man's name, and he offered to take me up to the mine, if I could manage a three-day walk through the wilderness.

The fact that he would not take any money impressed me. He did suggest that I pay for camping gear, which seemed fair. This included two pack dogs and a rifle, which I learned to shoot.

Mr. Braden and I left early one morning. He hired a native man to take us across the Copper River. That first day, we did not go far. Braden said I would need to get adjusted to walking.

Everything went smoothly until the third night out. I prepared myself for sleeping and had taken off my heavy outer clothing when Mr. Braden came at me very aggressively. He pulled me into his arms, kissing and fondling me. He was strong, but I fought him with all my strength, and managed to pull away. I was alarmed and frightened, but stood my ground. I demanded to know what he meant to do. He laughed and said that he had never known my brother. He just wanted me, and he meant to have me.

I was frantic. I felt utterly at his mercy. He told me to take off my clothes and yield to him. When I refused, he picked up his rifle, aimed it at me, and asked me if I would rather die than to give in to him. I knew that I would have to play his game. I tried to smile, and said I would rather be with him. I slowly began to unbutton my shirt, and so did he. But the moment he got his trousers half way down, I grabbed the rifle, which he had foolishly leaned up against a tree.

When he saw what I had done, he laughed and said that if I killed him, I would never find my way back. Then he rushed for me, and I pulled the trigger. He looked amazed as he fell.

He was gut shot, and did not die right away. It was horrible. He was in agony for a long time, and I did what I could for him. I wrapped him in his clothing and covered him with his blanket. When he was gone, all I had left were the dogs. I thought if I could get packs on them, they would lead me back to the river. But when I untied them, they ran away.

Now, I must try to make it on my own. I will take a knife and blanket, and as much food as I can carry. I will tie my red hair ribbon to this tree, and maybe someone will see it, find the box, and discover what happened here. God help me.

When I finished reading her note, I ached with compassion for this woman. Likely she never made it back. I put the tablet and the hairpins with the red ribbon into the tin box and stowed it with my gear.

I looked around for the remains of Todd Braden, but found nothing. Just as I was about to leave, I caught a glimpse of something shiny hidden in a patch of moss on the ground. It was a man's gold watch on a chain. On the back was engraved the initials, T B.

Weeks later, after finishing my work at the trapping cabin, I went to Copper Center and reported what I had found. Everyone was curious to see the red ribbon.

Mrs. Brown, owner of the roadhouse, remembered the lady. "It was a long time ago, when I first came here," she said. "She was looking for her brother, but I don't recall her name. She left with some man and didn't come back. That was not unusual. Most people were transient then. So we were not alarmed when we never saw either of them again."

The story found its way into the local newspaper, and later was picked up by a Seattle newspaper. By the time the story made it that far, it reported that I was mourning for the young lady, certain that she perished. This was embarrassing. But the story soon died out.

Two months later, I was surprised to receive a letter from Seattle with no return address. The handwriting looked familiar.

My Dear Mr. Wilson:

I am the lady who tied the red ribbon to the tree. It brought tears to my eyes when it was reported in the newspaper article that you had mourned for me. Thank you for feeling so kindly.

During all the years since then, not one day goes by without my remembering the terrible day when I killed Todd Braden. Standing there alone, depending only on myself, I felt a sense of strength I had never known before. My life up to then had been well-ordered, and I had always been cared for. Then, faced with a life or death situation, I had to take care of myself.

I had to get away from that place quickly. I knew the direction from which we had entered the camp. That's where I headed. The first day, I fought my way through the brush and trees until exhaustion overtook me. I wrapped myself in the blanket in a patch of moss and immediately fell asleep.

When I felt something warm moving beside me, I woke up screaming. It was the dogs. I was never so glad to see another living creature. I grabbed them around their necks and held them close. No one will ever know what those dogs meant to me.

The next morning, we came across a trail in the woods, and followed it all that day. Late in the evening, we came into a small native settlement. The people were as surprised to see us as we were glad to see them. They were very kind and took good care of us.

In the morning, I gave the dogs to the natives, but I cried when I said goodbye to them. Two young men rowed me across the river and walked with me to a roadhouse. It was not the one where I had stayed before, so no one knew me. I could tell that they were curious about my being with the natives, but no one asked any questions. I stayed there for a few days and then continued the search for my brother.

Two weeks later, I walked into the lobby of a roadhouse near Fairbanks and there he was! We were overcome with joy. He had not struck it rich, but he had enough money for our passage home.

Over the years, I often wondered if anyone would find the red ribbon. I was afraid that I might be hunted down and arrested for the murder of Todd Braden. Perhaps it could still happen, but for now, no one knows I still exist, but you.

Trustingly yours,
The Lady of the Red Ribbon

Sourdough Roadhouse

STUNNED, MARY BETH BACKED AWAY AND WHISPERED, "OH, LORD HELP ME! I DIDN'T KNOW THAT I WAS HIRED TO BE A . . . OH, I CAN'T EVEN SAY THE WORD!"

SAVING MARY BETH

IT WAS RAINING HARD THE DAY MARY BETH WAS FIRED FROM
the only job she'd ever had. Mrs. Hicks ordered Mary Beth to get
her things and leave, screaming at her, "Get out, get out!"

It hadn't taken long to pack her one little cardboard suitcase
with everything she owned. Mrs. Hicks was waiting for her at the
front door and said nothing as she handed Mary Beth her final pay.
Then she slammed the door so hard it almost hit Mary Beth

It had been a miserable morning. The furnace was not working,
the house was cold, breakfast was late, and the coffee was lukewarm.
Mrs. Hicks loudly blamed Mary Beth for everything that had gone
wrong. Mr. Hicks listened to the tirade for a few minutes, and then
spoke up in defense of the girl. This so infuriated Mrs. Hicks that
she flew into a rage and accused her husband of favoring Mary
Beth. The two quarreled until he fled to the shelter of his office,
and then Mrs. Hicks turned on Mary Beth. She accused her of
trying to "cozy up" to Mr. Hicks and continued to rant and rave,
scarcely taking a breath.

Unable to defend herself, Mary Beth began to cry. Mrs. Hicks slapped her and shoved her against the table. When Mary Beth tried to keep from falling, she accidentally knocked an expensive china cup off onto the floor, where it shattered. That was when Mary Beth was fired.

Mary Beth had worked in the Hicks house for six months after turning eighteen and being forced to leave the orphanage where she had lived all her life. She needed to support herself. She knew housework and taking care of babies, and the orphanage secured the job with Mrs. Hicks.

As Mary Beth stepped out onto the street, she was wet before she could open her old black umbrella. Not knowing what to do or where to go, she started walking toward downtown Seattle. When she came to a store with a sheltered entrance, she hurried under it to get out of the rain. She did not know how long she could stay there before the store owner would tell her to move along.

Being alone on the streets terrified her. She tried not to cry as she stood there shivering and wondering where she could go. Her life had been sheltered at the orphanage, and she had no experience in the outside world.

She watched as a fine horse-driven cab stopped in front of the store. A well-dressed man waited until his driver opened an umbrella for him. When he stepped down from the cab, he walked over to Mary Beth. As he approached, she felt a sense of fear and stepped back.

"Young lady, please do not be alarmed. I only want to be of assistance to you," he said gently. "I noticed that your clothes are wet from the rain, and that you're shivering from the cold. I have a daughter about your age, and I hope that if she were in distress, some kind person would help her."

Mary Beth was startled and speechless at first. She had been told not to trust strangers, but this man seemed kind and concerned for her. Because her situation was so distressing, she needed to trust someone. In a whisper, she said, "Oh, I just don't know what to do."

He replied, "My name is John Whitson. I want to help you."

In all her life, no one had ever said such words to Mary Beth. She was so overcome that she burst into tears for the third time that morning. She felt a little relieved from her sense of panic and despair and began to breathe more easily. But she couldn't hold back her tears.

"There, there, my child, don't cry. I have a home nearby where you can stay. You come along with me."

With that, he helped Mary Beth into his cab. They drove to a big house with a sign in front that read "Whitson Boarding House."

When the big front door opened, a rush of warm air enveloped Mary Beth. They walked into a large entryway where a young girl helped her remove her wet coat. In the spacious living room, a few young women were laughing and talking. As Mary Beth and Mr. Whitson entered, one woman stood up, and he said to her, "This young lady is Mary Beth. Please take care of her." Then to Mary Beth he said, "Gertie here will help you with all you need."

With that, he quickly turned and was gone before Mary Beth had a chance to thank him. Gertie laughed. "He's the boss here and he comes and goes without warning," she said. "Come on with me upstairs, honey, and we'll get you some warm clothes. You must be cold in those wet things. We'll get you dried out, and into a change of clothing, inside and out. When we have dinner, I'll introduce you to the other girls."

Gertie lovingly helped Mary Beth into new clothes, chatting all the time about nothing. After Mary Beth was dressed, Gertie said, "Now take the pins out of your hair, and I'll brush it for you."

When they finished with Mary Beth's hair, Gertie stood back and looked at the lovely girl. "My goodness," she said, "he really got a beauty this time. With your beautiful blonde hair and those deep blue eyes, you'll be a sensation."

No one had ever noticed what Mary Beth looked like before. It was a wonderful feeling to be admired. Gertie seemed so interested in her. She had no idea what Gertie meant when she said Mary Beth would be a "sensation" but she liked the sound of it. All she had ever done since the age of nine was to take care of babies at the orphanage. No one cared about her appearance. No one had talked to her except to give her orders. She longed for affection and when she hugged and loved the babies, she was scolded. With all of Gertie's attention and loving kindness, Mary Beth wondered if she were dreaming.

Dinner at the boarding house was fun. There was much talk and laughter, and everyone seemed happy. Four of the girls were anticipating with excitement a trip to Alaska. Mary Beth wondered what that was about. Gertie told her that Mr. Whitson would explain later.

Returning that evening, Mr. Whitson took Mary Beth aside and told her about the trip.

"These young women you've met are going to Alaska to work for me," he said. "Gertie takes care of them and all the details of the trip."

"Thousands of folks have gone to Alaska for the gold rush. Most of them land in Valdez, where I own a hotel that serves food, drinks, and entertainment. My girls live and work there. The pay is good and the girls have fun. If you would like to go, I would like to have you. I pay the traveling expenses. You live in my hotel. Then, after you start working, you pay me back what I have spent on you. My hotel is called Whitson's House."

Trying to take it all in, Mary Beth stuttered and nodded her head. "It all sounds too good to be true. Yes, I'd love to go and work for you."

With that, Mr. Whitson stood up. "Good girl. Gertie is my manager and will take charge of getting you girls ready to sail in two days. I'll see you all then."

The next two days were the happiest Mary Beth had ever been. The house was full of excitement as the young women prepared to sail for Alaska, the great, unknown land. It was exhilarating getting to know the other girls, who were full of fun and seemed to like her. The day of departure was a flurry of activity as the women boarded the ship, found their staterooms, and got unpacked. It was a day to remember for the rest of my life, Mary Beth thought.

The voyage up the inside passage took them through beautiful country. The ship sometimes moved so close to land that you could almost touch the trees on shore, or so it seemed. Mary Beth had never eaten such good food. She wished that the voyage would never end.

It was overcast the day they docked in Valdez, but the huge mountains that rose out of the sea were visible through the clouds. It seemed as if the entire population had come down to the dock to greet the newcomers. Mary Beth noticed that the crowd was all men, and wondered where the women were. She had not seen Mr. Whitson on the ship. When she asked Gertie about him, she was told that he never came to Alaska. He just recruited girls in Seattle to work for him.

"But don't worry your pretty little head about it," Gertie said. "I'm here to take care of all the details. You just follow me and smile a lot."

A fancy carriage pulled by two shiny black horses with red ribbons on their harnesses took the girls into town. The men seemed so happy and enthusiastic. Mary Beth was sure that she was going to like Alaska.

The carriage stopped at the Whitson's House Hotel. There were plenty of men to help the girls down from the carriage. One big man reached up and lifted Mary Beth down to the street, then hugged her tight. Mary Beth flushed with embarrassment.

"Why are these men so glad to see us?" she asked Gertie.

Gertie was busy organizing the girls. Their living quarters were on the ground floor behind the kitchen. Each girl was assigned to a small bedroom just big enough for two cots, and they all shared a bathroom down the hall.

After Mary Beth and her roommate, Martha, had unpacked, Gertie brought new dresses for them. Mary Beth expected a uniform of some kind for housework. But Gertie gave her a fancy, knee-length blue silk dress with short sleeves and a low neckline. Mary Beth was dismayed.

"Why would I wear a dress like that to do my work?" she asked Gertie.

"Now what kind of work did you expect to do?" Gertie replied.

"I thought I was to do housework."

"Well, that's not what we do. You are supposed to be an entertainer."

"Me? An entertainer? I can't sing or dance!" Mary Beth cried.

Gertie put her arm around the girl's shoulder and spoke to her in a low voice. "Honey, all you have to do is look pretty, smile your lovely smile, and dance with the customers. They will order drinks. Their drinks will be whiskey, but yours will be tea. The men like to have you drink and dance with them."

"I can't dance. I have never danced with a man in my life," Mary Beth protested.

"Well, you will be in good company. Most of the men can't dance, either. You just go down with the girls and see what happens. Maybe you can just talk to them. But I have to tell you, most of these men have been out in the mines for months, and they are lonely for the company of a girl—especially one as pretty as you."

The first man Mary Beth saw in the barroom was the big man who had lifted her down from the carriage. He rushed over and pulled her onto the dance floor. The music was loud and fast, and he whirled her around and around. She didn't even have to dance--all she had to do was try not to fall down! Then he took her to the bar, ordered drinks, and told her, 'They call me Big Jake around here, but you just call me Jake, and I'll call you Sweetie, 'cause you sure are a sweetie!' "

Mary Beth did not know what to say. Sitting there alone with a man was new to her. He seemed happy to have her company, and if this was to be her job, maybe it would be pleasant, she thought.

After more dancing and drinking, Jake said, "Sweetie, it's time to go upstairs."

Mary Beth looked startled and said, "Upstairs? Why?"

Jake gave out a big whoop, and laughed, "Don't you know what 'upstairs' means?"

"No, I don't know. I just got here this morning and I have not been upstairs," she said.

"My God, girl, didn't they tell you that you were supposed to please a man in the bedroom?" he blurted out.

Stunned, Mary Beth backed away from him and whispered, "Oh, Lord help me! I didn't know that I was hired to be a . . . oh, I can't even say the word! I have never been with a man, and I could never do that!" Tears formed in her eyes.

She began to run away, but Jake grabbed her hand and said, "Wait a minute. You mean to tell me that you did not know what the girls were supposed to do? Let's go to that table in the corner and talk about this."

After they sat down, Jake asked Mary Beth how she came to be with these girls. She told him about Mr. Whitson, and how he had helped her. She said, "When the girls talked about the hotel in Alaska, I assumed we would work in a hotel. I never dreamed I would be expected to be an entertainer until today, when Gertie gave me this dress. And please don't call me Sweetie, my name is Mary Beth."

"Well, little Mary Beth, they have got you obligated to them, and it will be a problem to get you out of their hands," Jake said. "Before they'll let you go, you'll have to repay them for your passage and keep. I suspect that you don't have any money to do that, and right now, I'm almost broke, too. I help support my mother who lives in Arkansas, and I just sent her most of my money. But I do have a small shack up the hill. You can stay there until I get enough money to pay your way out. Go get your things, and leave the dress. Go out the back way by the kitchen, and walk down behind the hotel. I'll meet you there. Mary Beth, don't tell anyone what you are doing, and—trust me—I will help you. You will be safe with me."

When big Jake Crawford left the hotel, he was completely sober. Finding a young innocent girl in such a situation disturbed him greatly. "What can I do for this helpless girl? I can't let her be ruined by a bunch of drunken miners like me," he told himself.

Jake left the hotel and made his way around the block to find food. You should stay hidden until I figure out what to do."

When they reached the shack, Mary Beth almost turned back. It was the sorriest structure she had ever seen. How could she live in such a place? But when they went inside, and Big Jake apologized for its shabbiness, Mary Beth said, "Please don't say that. I am so grateful for your help and a place to hide. Will you get into any trouble for helping me?"

"No, I don't think so, not legally, that is," Jake replied. "They will demand that you pay them back for the cost of bringing you to Valdez. Right now, I need to get some food and leave you to get settled in."

When he was gone, Mary Beth sat down on the rickety chair and looked around the room. A bunk covered with an assortment of motley blankets filled one wall. A small table was cluttered with unwashed dishes, and a bucket of water stood against the opposite wall. In the corner on a stack of bricks stood a Yukon stove. She wanted to cry. But she knew that would not help, so she got busy tidying up the shack. What else could she do? She had no choice but to trust Jake.

She didn't know him at all. He seemed kind and trustworthy. But so had Mr. Whitson. How long would she have to live in this place? When she thought of all that had happened to her since leaving the orphanage, she longed for the safety it had provided.

Before long, Jake returned with a pot of beans and a loaf of bread. At first there was little conversation. Then he explained that it would take some time for him to pay off Whitson. This news was more than Mary Beth could take, and she began to cry. Jake rushed to her and held her in his arms. He was tender with her. "Now, honey, don't cry. We will get this all taken care of and send you home where you belong. But for now, you'll just have to go along with me until I can work this out."

The next day, Big Jake went to see Gertie and told her what he had done with Mary Beth. Gertie was upset. "My gosh, Jake, what did you do that for? How can I explain this to Whitson? He will be down on me in a big way."

Jake asked her pointedly, "Why didn't she know what she was supposed to do when she got up here?"

Gertie protested. "I didn't know until I gave her that blue dress. I supposed that Whitson had told her, and that it was alright with her. This is something we girls do not discuss openly. But I can tell you that when Whitson doesn't get a payback from her, he'll raise hell with me. I am supposed to keep track of all these girls."

"How much will it take to pay Whitson off? Jake asked.

Gertie looked down at the floor and thought for a few seconds, then raised her head and said, "Over five-hundred dollars."

With that Jake stood up and started for the door. "That's a lot of money that I don't have."

The following day, one of Jake's friends stopped him on the street. "Hey, Jake, how did you make out with that gorgeous new little gal in blue at Whitson's last night?"

"Well, I didn't," Jake replied. "Turns out she got shipped up here by mistake, and had no idea what kind of work Whitson expected her to do. When I found out that she was innocent—a virgin-and horrified at the prospect of being one of Whitson's girls, I got her out of there. She's up at my place, and I've got to raise the money to pay off Whitson and send her home."

His friend spluttered in amazement. "I'll be damned. Imagine, a virgin in Valdez! I'd like to see her, but I'll throw in fifty bucks to help send her home." He handed Jake the cash.

The word spread quickly. Two weeks later, the men of Valdez had raised enough money to pay off her debt and send Mary Beth home to Seattle.

In the following days, while waiting for a ship to Seattle, Mary Beth was treated like royalty. She was a little virgin princess, and the men put her on a pedestal. When it came time to leave, they all came to the docks to see her off. Jake was the last to say goodbye, and when he took her hand, Mary Beth reached up and kissed his cheek. The men all whooped and cheered as Mary Beth walked up the gangplank. When the ship pulled away from the dock, the men watched and waved, but Big Jake was the only one who stayed until the ship was out of sight.

That was how Jake Crawford and the miners of Valdez saved Mary Beth from a life of prostitution.

かゝ • ⌒

Six months later, Jake knocked on the door of the home in Seattle where Mary Beth worked as a maid. When she opened the door, she almost fainted she was so happy to see him. Once again Jake picked her up off her feet and held her tightly.

After getting married in Seattle, Mary Beth and Jake moved to his home in Arkansas. With the help of Jake's mother, they raised eight children and lived happily for the rest of their lives.

DICK HEARD SOMETHING BEHIND
HIM. WHEN HE TURNED, A GREAT
BEAR WAS CHARGING. BEFORE HE
COULD MOVE, THE BEAR ROSE UP
AND RAISED ITS PAW. THAT WAS THE
LAST THING DICK REMEMBERED.

THREE BEAR STORIES

ANY TIME YOU HEAR A BEAR STORY, YOU HAVE TO WONDER IF
it has been embellished in the retelling. Each narrator wants his
story to be the most frightful one. The bear, of course, must be big
and ferocious, with huge claws and sharp teeth.

Well, I can't testify as to what the bears in the following
accounts looked like, because I never saw them. But anyone
who was living in the Copper River Valley in the 1920s will
remember two bear encounters—"Red" Hurst's (Bear No. 1)
and Dick Roland's (Bear No. 2). Bill Weir's story (Bear No. 3)
was not as well-known, but I believe the the essential facts are
correct.

BEAR NO. 1

Red Hurst was a little man with flaming red hair. He operated
the roadhouse at Chistochina, which he had helped build. He was
a quiet man. I don't think I ever heard him laugh. But he was a fine
host and cooked a real good pot of beans.

I will never forget the first time I stayed at the roadhouse. It was winter, and deep snow covered the land. The nights were extremely cold, with the thermometer hovering between forty and fifty below. The roadhouse was full of guests and the yard outside was filled with about thirty sled dogs and a female wolf.

My sister Aileen and I slept upstairs in a bed of unknown vintage. We had just climbed the stairs when a gust of wind shook that big log building. With a wind that strong, we knew we were in for quite a storm. The wind lulled a bit, but then about midnight it started up again with a vengeance, bringing with it a first-class blizzard. The snow was not falling down; it was blowing sideways across the window. We were thrilled, never having experienced such fury in a storm.

Outside, the wolf began a very low, mournful howl, and then all the dogs began howling. Their chorus and the sound of the blizzard blended in complete harmony. It was the greatest symphony I had ever heard on a night to remember.

By morning the storm had abated and all was calm. We went down to breakfast, and naturally all the talk was about the blizzard. Red, who usually did not talk much, could not help himself. "By gum," he said, "that was one of the worst things I ever saw in all my born days."

Everyone nodded in agreement, well almost everyone. Sam said, "Well, Red, I can think of something that happened to you that was worse than that storm."

"What was that?" Red asked.

"How could you ever forget that encounter with the bear? That was the worst thing that ever happened to you!" Sam replied, and he began to tell the story.

Red and two friends, Buck and Jake, were riding horseback near Chistochina. They were moving in single file, following a narrow path with thick woods on either side. Red was the last one in line. Suddenly, out of the brush charged a huge bear. He rose up beside the horse and with his huge paw took a swipe at Red's head. The blow displaced part of Red's scalp and knocked him off the horse. Red screamed in agony and lost consciousness as he fell. Just as quick as the bear had appeared, he disappeared.

As Red fell to the ground, Buck and Jake jumped off their horses and ran to help. Jake grabbed his rifle to ward off the bear if he returned, and Buck went to Red, whose head was bleeding. Buck knew he had to stop the bleeding, or else Red would die, so he pulled off his jacket and removed his cotton shirt to serve as a bandage.

The men were alarmed by the damage to Red's scalp, which hung to one side. Buck tried to pull it back into place while Red was unconscious. The shirt was not a very good bandage, but it helped slow the loss of blood. Red's friends were afraid for his life.

Between the two of them, they managed to lift Red onto Jake's horse behind the saddle, using Red's belt to tie him to the back of Jake's belt. On their way back to the roadhouse, Red began to moan and mumble. When they heard this, they were relieved. It seemed like a good sign. After they got Red into the roadhouse, they were able to bandage his head and stop the bleeding. Red was unable to stand and he could not stay awake. His friends were afraid he had a concussion. Neither man had any medical knowledge, but they knew they had to get Red to a doctor.

In those days, there was no road between Chistochina and Gakona, so the three men had to go on horseback about thirty miles to get to a car at Gakona. From there, they drove to Chitina, where a doctor came down from the Kennicott mine to examine Red. He determined that Red had no concussion. But he recommended that Red go to Seattle for surgery to put his scalp back in place.

So Red traveled to Seattle, a six-day voyage. He had been in the bush for so many years that when he got to the big city, the noise deafened him. He had never seen such traffic.

After the surgery, Red checked into the Atwater Hotel to await the departure of a northbound steamship. The nearest restaurant was on the other side of a busy street. Red stood on the curb, watching the traffic, afraid to venture into that stream of Model T Fords coming and going. He didn't know what to do until he saw a nun down the block starting across with twelve children. Red hurried over. The traffic stopped as the nun, the children, and Red crossed safely.

The trip to Seattle made a bigger impression on Red than the attack by the bear. Was he ever relieved get back to Alaska with all his beautiful red hair in place!

BEAR NO. 2

The next account is about what happened in 1928 to a young man named Dick Roland.

A native man came into Copper Center one day to report that Dick needed help. Dick couldn't walk. A bear had attacked him. Right away, four men—Paul White, John and Nelson McCrary, and Tommy Hike—volunteered to head up to Dick's cabin, where they found him in a pitiful condition. His legs were badly burned and he had not eaten anything but a chocolate bar and snow for a number of days.

Dick told his rescuers that he had just built a small fire in front of his cabin to smoke out the mosquitoes when he heard something behind him. When he turned, a great bear was charging. Before he could move, the bear rose up on its feet and raised its paw. That was the last thing Dick remembered.

When he regained consciousness, Dick felt terrific pains in his legs and head. Not only that, but the bear also had knocked him into his fire. Dick's legs were badly burned. Unable to stand, he crawled into his cabin. The pain was unbearable and he passed out from the agony. He was afraid that the blow to the side of his head had caused a concussion.

Unable to move, all he could find within reach was the chocolate bar. I Ie could reach some snow through a small crack in the wall. Thank God for that.

The men from Copper Center carried Dick up to see a doctor at the Kennicott Mine, who sent Dick to Seattle for specialized treatment. After surgery and much skin-grafting, Dick's legs were saved, and he was able to return to normal life.

Dick often wondered about three things: Why had the native man come to his cabin? He had never seen the man before. Why had he impulsively bought such a large chocolate bar? Why hadn't that patch of snow melted? He never found any of the answers, but had no complaints about the way things turned out.

BEAR NO. 3

Then there was Bill Weir. He had a different kind of bear story.

In the first place, Bill was quite deaf. You had to shout to make him hear. He lived close to Gakona in a little cabin, and we often saw him there when we went for mail. Bill was a pleasant man, but it was hard to talk with him because of his deafness. In the winter, we often took supplies to him with our dog team, as Bill did not have a team. But he did have a dog named Henry, a big yellow, short-haired creature of unknown breed. He could have been called a "hearing ear dog" if there were such a thing. Wherever Bill sat down, Henry sat right at his feet, never more than a foot away. When Bill moved, Henry moved.

We were all fascinated by Henry. We had never seen such an attentive animal. Bill told us that an old native man had fished the dog out of the river and given him to Bill. Henry was just a pup.

"Henry is my best friend," Bill said, "and I'll never forget the day he saved my life."

Of course, we urged Bill to tell us the story. He didn't say anything for a few minutes but called Henry closer to him and laid his hand on the dog's head while he told us about the encounter with a mother bear.

One day in July, Bill and his dog had been down to Gakona to get the mail and some supplies. On their way home, about one-hundred feet from the cabin, Henry stopped short. He moved in front of Bill and blocked the trail, letting out a low growl. Bill followed the dog's gaze and there, thrashing through the brush toward the cabin, was a mother bear with two cubs. Bill had not heard the noise. The sow had not seen them, either, until Henry's growl alerted her. When Bill started yelling, she and the cubs wheeled around and ran away.

Bill thought he owed his life to Henry.

When he finished his story and patted Henry affectionately, Bill announced, "This dog gets steak whenever I can get it for him. He's the best dog-friend a man could ever have."

Lower Tonsina Inn

JUST AS I WAS STRETCHING OUT
ON MY BEDROLL, PHIL SUDDENLY
PUT DOWN THE CATALOG,
REACHED UNDER HIS BUNK,
PULLED OUT A RIFLE, AND AIMED
IT IN MY DIRECTION.

☾ MOONLIGHT MADNESS

Slim Williams had the following experience, and I wrote it down just the way he told it to everyone who would listen.

"DANG BLAST IT, I'M ALREADY A DAY BEHIND SCHEDULE and now this trail goes rotten on me," I muttered to myself.

Me and my nine sled dogs had gotten a slow start because of trouble with the brake on my sled. By the time I got it fixed, I was just too plumb tired to pack up and leave. I had told Phil I would leave on Monday, and here it was Tuesday. My daylight would run out soon, but thank God there would be a full moon.

For those who don't know Alaska, it's not pitch dark up here all winter. When the moon is full and the skies clear, the bright moonshine reflecting on the snow makes for plenty of light. Not as good as sunshine, but better than the darkness of a moonless night.

The going had been easy until we reached an area where the edge of a small avalanche had almost obliterated Phil's good trail. I could still make out where it cut through the woods. The dogs, God love 'em, had been going strong, but now they wallowed in deep, drifted snow.

To mark the trail, I went ahead of the dogs on snowshoes and doubled back over my track. This took a lot of time, but it made for easier pulling, and I had to consider my dogs. I also unloaded about half my gear for a second trip. Even then, it was slow going.

As we mushed on through the night, as my mind wandered, I laughed about some of the things that happened to Phil and me on the trap line. Take cooking, for instance. Neither of us liked that job, so we traded off, each of us taking one week at a time. When Phil's turn came, he was like a bear, always growling about something. He would throw pots and pans around and cuss up a storm. One day I figured I would cure this behavior.

When it was my turn to cook, I acted just as he had, cussing, growling, and being unpleasant. He watched me for a long time without saying a thing. Finally, he said with a grin, "Is that the way I act, when I'm cook?"

Well, of course, I said, "yup." That was the end of his showing bad manners while cooking.

The dogs and I plodded on. I thought I might have to cache the rest of the load. The dogs were very tired and could hardly manage a small incline with me pushing. We rested there for a while and then slowly went on. I had never been to this particular trapping cabin of Phil's, so I didn't know exactly how much farther we had to go. Soon, however, we found ourselves back on Phil's good trail and the going was much better.

By this time, it was late into the night. We were about ready to take a rest when I got a faint smell of smoke. The dogs picked it up, too, and perked up. About then, Phil's dogs heard us and began barking. As the trail curved around a thick stand of spruce, we saw the cabin.

By now, all the dogs were barking and yipping, making a lot of noise. I could barely hear myself when I yelled out, "Hello the house!" as we pulled up in front of the cabin. No one came out, so I yelled again, "Hello the house!" Again, no response.

Because of the racket, I expected to see Phil come out and I was a bit alarmed when I didn't see him. How could he sleep? Before I could do anything else, I had to take care of my dogs. I took off their harnesses and tied them up in the clearing. Then, I gave all the dogs, including Phil's, pieces of dried salmon to keep them quiet. As they happily chewed their food I went into the cabin.

I expected to see Phil sound asleep on his bunk. To my surprise, he was wide awake, propped up against the head of his bunk, with a Sears & Roebuck catalog in his lap. He didn't say a word. He just sat there thumbing frantically through the pages. When he came to the last page, he began thumbing from back to front. It was an odd scene. I watched him for a moment or two, and said again, "Hello," but he ignored me.

The only light was a single candle on a table across the room from Phil. It was not giving enough light for him to see the pages he was turning. But he kept right on thumbing the catalog when I tried to talk to him. Being hungry, I opened a can of pork and beans and heated them on the wood stove. When I dished out a helping for Phil and set it in front of him on the table, he didn't even look at the food. No knowing what else to do, I ate, cleaned up, and then spread my bedroll on the floor across from Phil's bunk.

Phil's strange behavior was a puzzle. I had no idea what was wrong with him. I figured I would get some sleep and deal with the problem in the morning. Just as I was stretching out on my bedroll, Phil suddenly put down the catalog, reached under his bunk, pulled out a rifle, aimed it in my direction, and shot out the light of the candle next to me.

This scared the hell out of me. In the darkness, I heard him fooling with the rifle and held my breath until he put it away and climbed into his bunk. Only after he began snoring did I relax. Then, as quietly as possible, I crawled over to his bunk, reached underneath, and got the rifle. I laid it beside me against the wall, sighed, and quickly fell asleep.

The next morning, as soon as Phil stirred in his bunk, I was wide awake. I lay there watching to see what he would do. He didn't notice that I was there, so I kept quiet. He put on his boots and overcoat and went out the door. Then, I got up and was rolling up my bed when Phil came running in yelling, "Where's my gun, where's my gun? There's a pack of wolves out there, and I got to kill 'em all!"

He spotted his rifle on the floor where I had put it the previous night. Before I could do anything, he grabbed it and ran back outside. I was right behind. When he raised his gun to take aim at one of my dogs, I knocked him down before he could fire. He screamed as he fell, and I grabbed the gun out of his hand.

For a second I thought he was going to cry. He looked up at me and said, "What'd you do that for? I'm waiting for my partner, Slim, and I didn't want him to tangle with them wolves."

I helped Phil get up and told him to go inside. I would take care of the wolves. I wondered why Phil thought my dogs were wolves. I realized that his dogs were all housed along the side of a hill behind his cabin. He had fixed a place for my dogs along the side of the cabin across from the wood pile. When he came out and saw all those dogs so close together, I guess he thought he was seeing a pack of wolves.

Well, he went on back inside, and seemed to calm down, so I went in thinking I would cook breakfast. He was sitting on his bunk, thumbing through the catalog, and he paid no attention to me. I fixed some food, set it on the table, and told him to come and eat. But he ignored me and the food the rest of that day. By then I knew he had slipped a cog, and that I was in for some trouble. I'd had a little experience before with men who become crazy in the wilderness. They were dangerous and hard to handle.

I had never been much of a praying man, but this situation seemed to call for prayer. I wished I had learned to do it better. I knew I had to do something about Phil. If I went for help, I would have to leave him for at least two days. If I tried to take him on the sled, would he go peacefully? And there were his dogs to consider. I couldn't leave them, and I couldn't take them with me, so I decided to sit tight for a day or so and see what developed.

Try as I might to get Phil to eat something, he flat ignored me, and kept thumbing that dang catalog. Every once in a while he'd suddenly remember the wolves and run outside yelling for his gun. I'd give chase and managed to get him back inside and onto his bunk. Good thing I was a lot bigger than Phil. The third day, all of a sudden, Phil decided to eat and I had to stop him from gulping down his food and choking on it.

Then, the situation got worse. I went outside to get some wood, and he ran out behind me, grabbing the ax before I could stop him. He ran around yelling that he was going to chop the heads off those wolves. I picked up a long piece of firewood and threatened him with it, holding it over my head and ready to use it if I had to. He backed off a few feet, looked scared, and slowly laid down the ax. But he kept his eye on me. After a while, not saying a word, he turned and went back to his bunk and picked up the catalog, which was pretty well worn by this time. That evening, to my surprise, Phil put the catalog down with little prompting, and came to the table where he had a good meal.

I had hidden his gun and ax. The next morning as I was getting breakfast, Phil went outside. I watched him through the little window, not knowing what he would do next. When he returned, he walked over to the table, poured a cup of coffee, and raised it up to me. "Boy, Slim," he said, "it's sure good to see you. I been going nuts here by myself, but how come you were a day late? I looked for you all day yesterday. The last few days I've been busy getting things ready for you and your dogs. How was the trail?"

"Great," I replied.

Phil and I had a good trapping season that year. I never told him about his obsession with the Sears & Roebuck catalog and the wolves.

Many months later, I happened to encounter a doctor at the roadhouse, and asked him about Phil's strange behavior. It was probably a case of temporary insanity, he told me, caused by the depression of being alone and isolated.

Some people in these parts call this "moonlight madness."

AFTERWORD

IN 2001, AT AGE NINETY, I RETURNED TO THE COPPER RIVER country for the first time in decades, and have continued to spend each summer there since, enjoying old friends and making new ones.

Much has changed, of course, since I made it my home three-quarters of a century ago. Even though it is accessible by highway, the region remains one of Alaska's most unsettled places. But gone are the prominence of the roadhouses and the genial companionship they offered, replaced by fast cars and airplanes and by modern motels built to insure privacy rather than good company.

The huge old Tonsina roadhouse still stands, but it is quiet and lonely except for the good-natured ghost of Charlie who entertained me so long ago when I was a young girl new to the country. All the rooms but one are empty and cold now. The exception is Room 18, which the owners have kept furnished and in order, all these years for its long-dead occupant who claimed it as his own.

Only ruins remain of the original roadhouse at Paxson. I loved Paxson the best of all, as I met my first love there, John Meggett, the grandson of Dan Whitehead. I named my dog Paxson. Now, when I pass that old building just waiting to fall down, I remember how it felt to be in love for the first time, and I still smell the sweet potato pie that was a specialty of the cook. A new roadhouse was built across the road, but that is not where my heart lies.

Still standing and in good shape is the Gakona Lodge, even today reflecting the elegance of the workmanship of its Norwegian builders, Arnie Sundt and Herb Hyland. On the lawn is the old, rusted wagon, the very one on which I rode with Sundt up the frozen Copper River Valley in 1927, when he came a courting and my guardian turned him away because I was only fifteen.

The rest of the original roadhouses have burned or been bulldozed to make room for progress. The role they played in pioneering of Copper River Valley has been largely forgotten.

They were important to me because they offered shelter, friendship, hospitality, and, most important, a sense of home. Each one satisfied in some way that great need for companionship and camaraderie in this vast, remote country.

I shall never forget those old landmark roadhouses and the people who ran them.

READING RECOMMENDATIONS

for readers interested in books revealing the mysterious,
offbeat, and humorous side of life in Alaska

Fashion Means Your Fur Hat is Dead
A Guide to Good Manners & Social Survival in Alaska
Mike Doogan / $14.95

Moose Dropping & Other Crimes Against Nature
Funny Stories from Alaska
Tom Brennan / $12.95

Fishing for a Laugh
Reel Humor form Alaska
Lew Freedman / $14.95

Haunted Alaska
Ghost Stories from the Far North
Ron Wendt / $9.95

How to Speak Alaskan
Mike Doogan / $4.95

Strange Stories of Alaska & the Yukon
Ed Ferrell / $14.95

What Real Alaskans Eat
Not Your Ordinary Cookbook
J. Stephen Lay / $12.94

EPICENTER PRESS
Alaska Book Adventures™ • www.EpicenterPress.com

ABOUT THE AUTHOR

SAMME GALLAHER LIVED IN the wilderness of the Copper River Valley for two years when she was a teenager. Her experiences there are still vivid in her memory some eighty years later, at age ninety-seven. The author spends summers in Alaska and lives most of the year with her niece and family in Thousand Oaks, California.